BROKEN BABY

SUGAR BABIES #2

CHARITY PARKERSON

--Warning: This book is intended for readers over the age of 18.

Copyright © 2019 Charity Parkerson
Editor: Hercules Editing & Consultants
ISBN: 978-1-946099-51-8

INTRODUCTION

LANE HAS HIS SHARE OF ADDICTIONS. WALKER
IS ONE.

After months of rehab, Lane finally feels like life is headed in the right direction. Between starting his own business and helping out Trace with Club Incubus, his bank account is looking fantastic too. His friendship with Walker gets deeper every day. Until Lane looks over one day and realizes he's in love with the guy.

Walker never expects to fall for someone half his age, especially someone like Lane. For a long time, Walker didn't even like the guy. After months of visiting doctors together, getting Lane's life on track, now Walker is the one who needs help. The only difference is, Walker has no intention of dragging Lane into his problems. Lane just finished rehab. Walker can't disrupt his life. It's too bad Walker ends up crushing Lane in the process of keeping him at arm's length.

Can these two men meet in the middle while both on shaky ground? Lane is up for the challenge. If only Walker would let him in.

ONE

INVENTORY TIME at Club Incubus sucked big time. Unless Walker was making plans to spend the entire day alone with Lane, trapped elbow deep in liquor, and with no one else around. That was a scenario Walker could get behind. He desperately wanted to get behind Lane.

The scent of Lane's cologne kept wafting Walker's way. Walker caught himself leaning closer to the scent. It was only the tenth time it happened. Walker swore the space between them got smaller by the second. He wasn't entirely sure he was the only one moving closer. At some unnamed point in the past year, Walker had fallen for Lane. It was crazy. It was equally stupid. Lane was straight... possibly. Truthfully, he'd never seen Lane date anyone at all, even though the guy flirted with everyone—men and women. Not that it mattered. Walker couldn't be with him. The man's friendship was as close as Walker would ever get to having Lane.

"Tomorrow, we'll start on the stock rooms. It'll be easier if the place is closed while we work."

Lane smiled.

Walker forgot his place. If Lane realized Walker simply rambled just to be close to him, he didn't let on. With his brain fixated on musing over the softness of Lane's lips, Walker fell into a detailed list of things they needed to do to get ready for him to be on vacation for a while. He needed to teach Lane how to keep Club Incubus running in his absence. All Walker could think about was Lane looked like he'd fit perfectly against Walker's chest.

He hadn't meant for this to happen. His boss and the owner of Incubus, Trace, had married Lane's dad. He'd also taken up the role of helping Lane get his life together. Since Walker loved Trace and wasn't heartless, he'd also chosen to help. They'd been to appointment after appointment, getting Lane clean while testing for different ailments. Since Lane's drug addiction had begun as self-medicating for a mystery illness, it hadn't been easy finding a diagnosis. They'd done it together. Unfortunately, while Lane had been focused on his health, Walker had been completely focused on Lane. One day, when he hadn't been looking, Lane had burrowed beneath his skin. He couldn't see anything else.

"You might want to wear something you don't mind ruining tomorrow. Some of the boxes in the back are pretty dusty." He brushed a nonexistent wrinkle from Lane's chest.

Lane's hand covered Walker's, holding it against his heart for half a second before he seemed to realize what he'd done. His hand fell away. A soft chuckle caressed Walker's ears. He couldn't look away from Lane's lips. "Should I expect to end up on my knees? Crawling through the maze of liquor crates back there," Lane clarified. The wicked smile stretching his lips said Lane knew exactly what image sprang to Walker's mind.

Walker shrugged. "I mean, I won't stop you if you want to get on your knees. These floors are pretty dirty, though." The way Lane's eyes flashed with good humor kept Walker talking shit. He couldn't recall a word he'd said a half second after it left his lips. He'd never wanted someone so badly it made him stupid. Lane was a first for him in a lot of ways. Walker wished he could be a first for Lane too. Damn, he had it bad.

SWEET BROWN EYES HELD LANE CAPTIVATED. It helped or hurt, depending on how Lane looked at things, that those eyes swam with laughter. Lane had no clue what Walker talked about. Lane reacted to Walker's story by mimicking his mood. If Walker smiled, Lane smiled. If he laughed, Lane did too. Otherwise, he couldn't make his brain focus with Walker standing so close. They'd known each other a long time. Lane's body had never reacted like this to the man until recently. Since he'd left rehab eight months ago, Lane looked at Walker differently. They were no longer the enemies they'd once been nor were they friends. Walker obviously thought of Lane as a friend. Lane was the one having trouble staying in his lane.

"Are you cool with staying late tonight or are you too tired?"

Lane forced himself to focus. "I'm good. Let's get these receipts done and then we'll be good to take stock tomorrow."

Humor flashed in Walker's eyes. "That's what I just said."

Oops. "Yeah. Just repeating it so you know I'm listening." Fuck. Walker made him a mess. This was stupid. He'd never dated a guy. To be fair, Lane didn't date anyone. He'd been too busy getting fucked up during the pivotal years most people spent playing the field. Lane had just been trying to survive. He flirted with people, men and women, for the fun of it, because he like making people smile. Otherwise, nothing. It was like that part of his brain was broken. He just didn't feel moved by anyone. No one aroused him. Walker moved him. It was fucking odd. The guy had even told Lane once he wasn't interested in him. He should shut this down. "I guess I'd better help count out some registers so we can get started."

Walker rapped his knuckles on the bar. "Good idea. I'll start on the other side."

Lane watched Walker as he crossed the room to the other bar. He was so big. Tall. Muscular. Lane felt scrawny. Addiction had done that too. He'd gained a little weight in the past year of clean living but not much. He turned away, feeling self-conscious. Even though Lane had started his own business, and he still worked for Club Incubus, he didn't have much to offer. His finances being good didn't mean much. Lane was still a recovering addict with Fibromyalgia and had more bad days than good. He'd lived in severe pain for years before his diagnosis. Finding out the cause of his mystery pains hadn't brought relief. It didn't matter men often slipped through the cracks when it came to a Fibro diagnosis since it was more common with women. He could've stayed lost in the cracks and nothing would've changed—other than people no longer thinking he was crazy or just looking for prescription drugs. Doctors had no real way to treat his problem. There was no cure. All the doctors could do was try to make it bearable, so Lane still suffered. Only now, he writhed in pain on his bad days while racked with guilt because he wanted to go back to the only relief he'd known—addiction. His life wasn't much worth living. Lane didn't imagine anyone would want to spend theirs with him, getting dragged down.

With that depressing knowledge weighing him down, Lane pasted on a fake smile and moved to help Summer close out her register. Club Incubus and its staff was the only real home and family he had anymore. His mom had passed years ago and his father recently remarried. It was odd that he now had a stepfather younger than him. Not that Lane cared. Trace owned Incubus. He'd given Lane a job and funded the startup of his dispensary. Paid for his rehab and counseling. Without Trace, he'd still be in a drug-fueled haze somewhere. Lane didn't know some days if he should thank the guy for saving him or not. It didn't always feel like a rescue. Sometimes it felt more like a life sentence. Dragging his brain from the depths, Lane focused harder on his task, helping Summer count out her register.

"You're probably ready to go home."

Summer winked at Lane's observation. "You know it. Zoe just texted me that she's going to bed, so I know it's warm and waiting, you know?"

Lane chuckled to hide his jealousy. His bed would be cold as always. "How is Zoe?"

Zoe and Summer had been dating for two years. At one point, Zoe had also worked for Incubus, but Trace didn't allow employees to date each other. Working together in a nightclub and dating didn't mix. Everyone flirted with staff. That didn't mesh well with relationships. But Summer and Zoe were the real thing. They'd chosen each other over a job. Summer had stayed because she made more than Zoe. Lane had no clue what Zoe did now.

"She's doing good," Summer said, opening her register and pulling out bills. "Business is good here, so my tips are paying the bills. I mean, we struggle, but she wanted to go back to school and it'll be worth it someday."

Lane flashed her an understanding smile. "The things we do for love, eh?"

She chuckled as she pulled her long blond hair up into a ponytail. Her blue eyes flashed with mischief. "You say that as if you'd know. I don't think I've ever heard any rumors about your personal life. Are you keeping someone on the side? If so, tell me everything."

Her conspiratorial tone was too much. Lane couldn't help himself. "I'm part of a harem, didn't you know? The seven of us live together. When our mistress doesn't see us for a while, we spend all our free time pleasuring each other. I never talk about it, because," Lane shrugged, "I don't like making people jealous."

A loud snort escaped Summer. She covered her mouth and nose, trying to stifle the sound. "You're outrageous. Please tell me every word of that is true. I want to be the one who tells everyone."

"Nah," Lane said, picking up the bills and flipping through them, ensuring they each faced the same way. "I'm boring. I work here at night and keep an eye on my dispensary during the day. It runs without me, but still. There's no time for dating."

Summer leaned on her elbows on the bar and held Lane's stare. "Someone once suggested that I stop saying I don't have time for things. Instead, I should say I don't make things a priority. If I can say that and not feel like shit about it, then I'm doing right by myself and others. If not, then I'm not being true to myself and the people in my life, because there's always time. We just make a mental note of how to spend ours each day. I didn't realize how true it was until I tried it. Try it."

Lane stopped fidgeting with the money. "Dating isn't a priority to me."

"Huh," Summer said, holding his stare. "I guess it really isn't. That sounded true to me."

Lane added Walker to the mix in his head. *Dating Walker isn't a priority to me*. Great. That didn't sit well.

Thankfully, Summer had moved to finishing their work. She counted each stack and made notes of her figures. Lane double checked her count. They both signed off on the numbers. Lane tried to be as quick as possible without making mistakes so Summer could get home.

"Thanks, Summer. I think you're free to go."

"Cool. See you tomorrow night," she said with a final wave as she headed for the door.

Lane caught Mason's eye and nodded his way, letting the bouncer know it was time to walk

Summer to her car. They didn't let any of the bartenders or servers walk to their cars alone. The world was a crazy place. With one register down and three to go, Lane moved on without giving in to temptation to look Walker's way. Sometimes, he swore he felt the man's stare, but he'd never caught Walker at it. Lane imagined it was simply wishful thinking. After all, who could ever love someone like him?

It was oddly comforting sitting inside Incubus after closing time. All the flashing lights were gone. The loud music had long past died away. It was as if the building had pressed pause, waiting for the next night of partygoers. Its wooden bars and dance floor smelled like lemon polish. This place felt more like home than Walker's two-bedroom apartment. After all, he was here more than he was there. That would change soon. One more day of work, and then he'd be off for at least five months. Lane didn't know yet. He just thought Walker was going on vacation next week. More than likely, Trace would tell Lane the rest after that.

"Did the place seem busier tonight than usual, or am I imagining things?"

Walker blinked hard, trying to focus. "It was busier. Dillion came in with some guy who is YouTube famous. Apparently, the guy announced online where he'd be." Not to mention, Dillion was super famous and every single gay man in a hundred-mile radius always showed where he did. Dillion was a regular. He was young and beautiful. Dillion was also dramatic, and Walker always chose to steer clear. In fact, if not for Trace, Walker might've banned the guy months ago.

The receipts spread across the table blurred again. Walker squeezed his eyes closed. His head pounded. Things were getting worse. He was exhausted. Even Walker's arms felt heavy. A warm weight leaned into his side. Cologne like spicy chocolate overwhelmed him. A smile touched his lips. Lane's cologne wasn't strong-smelling. It was like Walker was more in tuned to Lane than anyone else.

"Are you falling asleep on me?"

Walker's smile grew at Lane's question. "If I fell asleep on you, I'd crush you." Lane was so skinny. Walker was solid. He'd always had a large frame and had to stay in shape to keep from going to fat. Walker didn't doubt for a second he'd suffocate Lane in a matter of minutes if he dozed off on top. Damn, Walker's mind always went straight to sex when it came to Lane. He'd been celibate too long. At some point, Walker realized no one would do but Lane. He hadn't slept with anyone since.

"Would I die with a smile, though? I mean, that's the real question, right?"

Walker snorted. He loved that Lane was always up to flirt, even if it meant nothing. "You wouldn't know what to do with me."

Lane leaned even closer. He set his chin on Walker's shoulder and looked up at him from beneath his lashes. "You could teach me, Daddy. I'll do whatever you say."

Walker went hard. Lust tightened his entire body, making his skin too tight. It didn't matter Lane played around and didn't mean a word. Walker craved. He tried laughing it off while hiding his erection. "You don't have an obedient bone in your body."

"I have one." Lane's instant transformation to serious had Walker holding his stare. Electricity popped between them. There was no way Lane didn't feel the same connection Walker did. "You look tired."

Lane's claim brought Walker back to reality. He couldn't be with Lane. Not right now. Walker pasted on a fake smile. "I'm getting old, babe. Staying up late every night is a young man's game."

Lane straightened. "We could always finish this tomorrow, after we've had some sleep."

At just the mention of sleep, exhaustion washed over Walker. "Trace will be here in the morning. If we leave him a note, letting him know where we left off, he can finish this."

"Wow," Lane said, sounding shocked. "I never thought I'd live to see the day you'd go for my suggestion to leave early. You must really be tired."

Walker weakened by the second. He was a little scared he might not make it home. "Yeah. Sorry. Maybe I'm coming down with something."

Lane's gorgeous green gaze swept Walker's face and filled with concern. He stood. "Come on. My place is closer and I'm not sure you should be driving."

A soft chuckle escaped Walker. "I'm way too fucking big and old to crash on your couch. Two hours in and I'd need a good chiropractor."

"We're adults. My bed is big enough for two." Lane's expression remained clear, as if he really believed they could share a bed, no issue.

Fuck it. He was tired. "Okay." Yeah, that was his voice, agreeing to go to bed with Lane... and sleep.

Thankfully, his body gave out before they made it to Lane's. His head bobbed, waking him several times before they circled Lane's store to the back to his apartment. Every step he took toward the door felt like it was made through quicksand. He worried he wouldn't make it to the bed. The apprehensive glances Lane shot his way made Walker wonder how bad he looked. If he looked a quarter as poorly as he felt, then Walker imagined he looked pretty fucking terrible.

Once they cleared the door, Walker headed straight for the bedroom. He'd been to Lane's apartment countless times. It felt like a second home. Lane suffered from Fibromyalgia and the journey they'd taken to get that diagnosis had been a long one. Walker had sat at Lane's side, suffering with him through flare-ups while doing everything in his power to try to relieve the pain. Now those days and nights came to his rescue. Lane didn't care Walker was currently stripping and climbing into his bed.

Lane killed all the lights but a soft salt lamp he kept on his dresser. Walker watched him through half-closed lids. He moved around the room, gathering Walker's discarded clothes and finding clothes for himself. Lane slipped from the room. Sleep carried Walker away. The bed dipped beside him, dragging Walker from a dream he forgot immediately. Even though it was dark and the room was unfamiliar, Walker knew he was with Lane. Nothing else mattered. Halfway between asleep and waking, he rolled and molded against Lane's back. With his arm draped over Lane's waist, he towed the man tighter against his chest. Lane didn't protest. Walker was more asleep than awake. It was like part of a dream. Lane seemed to snuggle against him— like getting comfortable or savoring Walker's touch. Without thought, Walker's lips brushed the shell of Lane's ear. His palm found Lane's heart and stayed. The steady beat against his hand proved the love of his life lived. This time, when sleep stole Walker away, he went feeling safe in the knowledge that he held the world.

TWO

FOR THE TENTH TIME, Lane squeezed past Walker as they worked inside the small stockroom. His chest moved along Walker's back. His hips brushed Walker's ass. Walker could barely breathe. Lust owned him. Since he'd woken with Lane draped over him like a blanket, Walker's dick wouldn't rest. He'd pretended to sleep while Lane sneaked from the bed, obviously hoping Walker wouldn't realize how they'd slept. Walker hadn't stopped twitching in his jeans since. He hoped his gaze didn't appear half as hungry as it felt while following Lane everywhere he went. For fuck's sake, Lane had washed and dried Walker's clothes before coming to bed so Walker would have something clean to wear today. How was he supposed to resist someone like that? He couldn't stop eating Lane alive with his eyes. Unfortunately, Trace kept catching him staring. Thankfully, Lane did not. Walker could deal with Trace's knowing smirks.

Walker tore his gaze away from Lane's ass for the hundredth time as Trace rounded the corner. He flashed his tiny, sexy boss a wink as he passed. The moment his back was turned, Walker was right back to feasting on the sight of Lane. The craziest part was, it wasn't Lane's looks that turned on Walker. Lane was gorgeous with his blond hair and green eyes. But that wasn't what did it for Walker. It was the man's vibe. His gaze always flashed with intelligence. Lane's mind was gorgeous. He was the smartest person Walker had ever met. Lane could hold his own in any conversation. Most of all, he was brave, and when he smiled at Walker, Walker felt like he'd won the damn lottery.

Lane spun. Their gazes met. Lane smirked. The way he always did—like he could read Walker's thoughts. "So you haven't said what you'll be doing with all your banked vacation time. Are you going somewhere exotic? I'm already sad I won't get to see you for a while. Should I be jealous too?"

"I don't know. Have you ever been to Disney in Orlando?"

Lane tilted his head to one side as if he needed to think it over. "No. I believe I might've gone to the one in California when I was really little, but my mom's health started failing when I was eleven, and you know." Lane shrugged.

"The one in Cali is cool, but you need to go to the one in Orlando. It's awesome. You should come with me and do the extreme challenge."

"There's an extreme challenge?"

Walker nodded. "See, there're four parks. Together, they have forty-eight thrill rides. The extreme challenge is doing all forty-eight in one day."

Lane pulled a face. "Is that even possible?"

Walker shrugged. "You have to go at a certain time of year. Plus, you need to stay at one their hotels so you can take advantage of extended hours for hotel guests. Even still, I've tried three times and only done it once. There's a science to it, but it's a blast trying. You should come with me."

"Seriously?"

"Why so disbelieving?"

Lane shook his head. "Sorry. I just figured you had a ton of other people you'd rather go with."

It hit Walker. After all the months of phone calls

through Lane's rehab, and all the time spent together, Lane still didn't believe Walker was his friend. That was probably the only reason Lane hadn't asked why Walker would be off for so long. He didn't believe he had any right. "There's no one else I'd rather go with. So come with me. I already have a room booked on site. You won't even have to pay for that."

"I can't take off the same time as you. That would leave Trace shorthanded. Otherwise, I'd love to go. It sounds fun."

"Go," Trace said, reminding Walker of his presence. "Hunter and I can run this place without you for a week. Plus, you really should take your vacation now. With Walker being out for so long, you'll probably be limited on what days you can take off."

Lane's gaze moved between Trace and Walker. He looked hopeful. Walker's excitement grew. He decided to push harder. "Please, Lane. I don't like going alone."

Lane bit his bottom lip, but his smile still peeked through. "I mean, my store runs itself, so I'm not really needed there." Walker smelled victory. "Okay," Lane finally said, making Walker fight the urge to happy dance. "Do I need to book a flight or..."

Walker dug out his phone and pulled up his

flight info. "I'll snag a ticket for you on the same flight as me." He barely stopped himself from bouncing in place. They were going on a trip together. Nothing would happen between them. That wasn't an option, but just the idea of a week alone with Lane had him ready to crow. He'd been trying to mentally prepare himself not to see Lane for a while. Now they had a whole week alone. He couldn't wait.

"Let me know how much I owe you."

"*Pssh*." Walker didn't bother saying anything past his dismissive noise. Lane wasn't paying for this trip. Soon enough, money would get tight for Walker. For now, he could do this. One last hurrah. What did money matter anyhow? He couldn't take it with him.

***

THIS WAS HELL. A SOLID WEEK OF BEING ALONE with Walker had Lane on the verge of a mental breakdown. Each accidental brush of skin, lingering look, and night of sleeping feet apart made Lane question if they could be friends anymore. Walker treated him like he should—like friends. Lane was the one having a hard time separating the way he felt from reality.

"I'm sorry. I have to say this. This has been amazing. I've had so much fun. This place is beautiful. That jack-in-the-box outside our room is fucking disturbing."

A sexy-sounding chuckle escaped Walker. He peeled off his shirt and unbuttoned his jeans. Walker spoke to Lane as if he wasn't killing Lane while stripping. Lane wondered if he would scream or cry because it was almost over. "Are you still glad you came?"

Lane tore his gaze away from Walker's massive bare chest and focused on his sweet brown eyes. Funny how that wasn't better. "Absolutely. Ten stars. Would recommend. Thank you for letting me tag along. Sorry we didn't beat the extreme challenge."

Walker climbed onto his bed, balled up his pillows, and collapsed onto his back. In his boxers. Lane couldn't breathe. "Meh. I knew it was a long shot this year since it's summer. It's a lot busier this time of year and we forgot to fast pass some popular stuff. It was still a blast trying, though. I'm also pretty sure I gained at least five pounds from all the times we stopped to grab snacks."

Lane settled on his side. He felt young for the

first time in forever. It had been fun. Damn, Walker looked tan and sexy. "*Mmmm*, those crispy rice, marshmallow, and chocolate mouse ears. Yum. But I'm pretty sure anytime you gain weight, it shows up as muscle. Every pound I gain shows up on my stomach."

A sexy-sounding snort left Walker. "You're so tiny. I'm convinced fat refuses to stick to you." Walker let out a jaw-cracking yawn. There were dark circles under his eyes. Lane had noticed Walker losing steam throughout the week. They'd ended up back at the room earlier and earlier each night.

"I think you needed this vacation. You look tired."

"Just what every guy wants to hear," Walker said, smiling. He closed his eyes. "I'm burned out." The admission surprised Lane. Walker seemed invincible. "That's why I'm taking so much time off. All the late nights have kicked my ass." His voice got softer with each word. His breathing deepened. The lights and the TV were still on. Lane didn't move. He was too fascinated by the sight of Walker. This was his last chance to watch him like this. There was no one there, forcing him to cast glances on the sly. With Walker sleeping, Lane could stare and dream. He had no idea how much time passed, nor did he care. Walker wouldn't be at Incubus for a while. Lane had millions of questions, but he was too scared to ask. He feared he'd learn they weren't really friends when Walker told him it wasn't his business. Lane would miss him, though. He missed him already.

Walker's body jerked in his sleep. A low moan slipped from his lips. Lane's eyebrows lifted. His gaze sharpened. As he looked on, barely blinking, Walker's nipples hardened. An erection tented his boxers. Lane's eyes burned from lack of blinking. Walker's dick peeked out from the slit in Walker's boxers. Saliva filled Lane's mouth, forcing him to swallow. He'd never seen Walker's cock. In truth, Lane hadn't expected his body's reaction to the sight. Lane had a dick. He could play with it anytime he wanted. This was different. Lane's entire body was taut. His desire to see more was overwhelming to the point his brain itched. He massaged his erection through his underwear, trying to ease some pressure while feeling like the biggest of pervs.

From his spot on the bed, Lane stared and craved. The sexy moan didn't come again. Lane couldn't tear his eyes away from Walker's semi-hard dick peeking out from his boxers. His entire body hummed with desire. He wanted to scratch off his skin. It had been years since anyone turned him on. Back in his teenage years, his best friend had been a girl. The more time they'd spent together and they closer they'd gotten, Lane had found himself slowly feeling things for her. He'd never really fantasized about anyone before her or since. While Lane had always known he wasn't like other people, he hadn't realized there was a name for people like him until he'd gotten older. Since then, he'd kept a wall between his friends and himself. He made friends, but he didn't intentionally get close unless he knew they had a shot at becoming more. Lane hadn't meant to feel anything for Walker. He definitely hadn't intended to end up lusting after him. Yet, here he was.

Another slight moan filled the air. Walker's cock became firmer. More saliva filled Lane's mouth. His dick leaked, soaking his underwear. The craziest thoughts entered his head with barely any blood making its way to his brain. This might be the only chance he got. If he didn't make his move now, he might never have another chance. As he eased from the bed, Lane questioned his sanity. They were thousands of miles from home. If Walker shot him down, they'd have to fly back home together under extremely awkward circumstances. Walker was worth the risk. Plus, Lane couldn't fight his desire any longer. There were only two steps between their beds. As Lane reached Walker's side, Walker rolled, facing Lane. His cock slipped even more from his underwear. Lane's gaze moved from Walker's dick to his sleeping face and then back again. Since he wasn't the type to sit around indulging in sexual fantasies, he hadn't thought about what it might be like to rub his erection against someone else's. Lane hadn't imagined licking someone's dick. He wanted to do those things with Walker. Before he could stop himself, Lane traced a thick vein in Walker's cock with his fingertips. Walker moaned again. Lane froze. Walker didn't stir. Lane dropped to his knees. He had to know. Just one taste. A huge part of him hoped Walker woke and wanted more—wanted Lane. If he got shot down, it might just kill him. For a long moment, Lane stared hard at Walker, willing him to wake. He didn't. Lane couldn't take the temptation any longer. He leaned closer. His heart pounded in his ears. The front of his underwear was soaked with pre-cum. His cock twitched, ready to blow without a single stroke. As he looked on, a drop of pre-cum dripped from Walker's cock. Lane's breath stuttered from his lungs. His tongue shot out, capturing the salt. Lane's eyes fell closed with ecstasy as his tongue circled Walker's crown, searching for more. Walker shifted restlessly. Lane's gaze shot to his face. Walker's eyes never opened. His breathing returned to normal. Lane's tongue found Walker's crown again. This time, he applied more pressure, licking only the tip. He liked it. Lane kissed Walker's cock and then opened his lips over the crown. He sucked lightly. A louder moan filled the air. Lane's dick pulsed. Walker's fingers found his hair.

"*Mmmm*, Dillion."

Lane froze at the muttered words. Pain sliced through him. He shot to his feet and made a beeline to the bathroom. Lane closed himself inside and tried catching his breath. He was such an idiot. Why had he done that? It was like all the years of drug use had completely fried his brain. He'd known there was no way in hell Walker could possibly want him. Yet he'd done that stupid shit while Walker dreamed about someone else. Lane's gaze locked on his reflection. He looked as wrecked as he felt. His dark blond hair and green eyes looked like thousands of other people's. There was nothing special about him. He hadn't known Walker had a thing for Dillion. It was possible the two were dating. Lane's heart cracked.

Dillion was beautiful. Lane didn't need to be gay

to see that. Dillion had very boyish features and carried himself with confidence. Not to mention, he had money and sass. Lane had nothing. His business was doing well, and his bank account looked very nice, but he had too much baggage. Fibromyalgia had him down more days than he liked, and rehab wasn't so long ago. No one would ever want him. He'd been a fool to take a chance. Now he couldn't go back to being only friends. It was good that Walker was leaving Incubus for a few months. Lane would give his notice too. It was time he moved on from Walker and that place. He couldn't stay knowing what he'd just done. His heart couldn't take the pain.

WALKER STARED AT THE CLOSED BATHROOM door, willing it open again. He had no idea why he'd just done that. Well, that wasn't completely true. He'd woken from a dream about Lane. A quick peek Lane's way had proven the man watched him sleep. He'd looked so goddamn turned on that Walker hated closing his eyes against it. Lane's expression also made Walker wonder what he'd said in his sleep.

He'd closed his eyes and pretended to sleep. His dick had other plans. It knew Lane was there as it had this entire trip. Each time he sneaked a glance Lane's way, he'd looked even hornier than last time Walker looked. Walker found himself trying harder to lure Lane into giving him a show. Instead, Lane had done something he'd never expected.

The instant Lane's tongue touched his cock, Walker nearly came. He'd never fought so hard to fake sleep in his life. Lane hadn't stopped. Walker panicked. He'd known he'd eventually have to acknowledge what was happening because he was going to blow, and no way could he pretend to sleep through that. So, he'd done the only thing he could think to do—he'd crushed Lane.

Now Walker couldn't stop staring and waiting. His every muscle was so tight, he wondered if he'd snap a tendon. By the time the bathroom door re-opened, Walker was ready to kick it down. Lane's head didn't turn Walker's way as he headed back to bed. It didn't matter. Walker could feel the pain rolling off Lane in waves.

"Lane, are you okay?"

Lane crawled beneath the covers and faced the wall before answering. "I'm good. Go back to sleep."

Walker settled on his side and stared at Lane's outline beneath the covers. His chest hurt. His eyes burned. Dillion was the last goddamn person on the planet Walker would ever want. He'd just been the first name that came to mind. If Lane knew Walker at all, he'd realize that. Walker rubbed his chest. As long as he lived, he'd never forgive himself for this night. The thing was, he might not have long to live with it, and Walker couldn't put Lane through anything else.

THREE

CONSIDERING everything Walker was currently
going through, Lane probably shouldn't be the only
thing on his mind. Actually, it was the lack of Lane
in Walker's life that he couldn't stop obsessing about.
In Orlando, Walker had woken to find Lane packed
and ready to leave. He'd barely looked Walker's way
and kept his earbuds in the whole way home,
avoiding any chit chat. Walker hadn't heard from
him since. He'd tried texting. No answer. In a
desperate reach, Walker had called Trace, hoping for
any news at all. Any little detail at all about Lane's
life was better than nothing. Instead, he'd learned
Trace was out of town and the club was
shorthanded. Walker hadn't hesitated to volunteer.
That was how he'd ended up there—back at Club

Incubus for the night with Lane openly ignoring him.

For what felt like the hundredth time, Walker found a reason to be where Lane was—the office, the bar, and in the VIP lounge. Each time he found an excuse to be within three feet of Lane, Lane found a reason to move away. He wouldn't even look at Walker. Walker resorted to sneaking up on him.

While Lane's head was down, helping count out Summer's register, Walker crowded Lane against the edge of the bar. He molded against Lane's back. "Excuse me," Walker said close to Lane's ear as he reached past him and grabbed a forgotten towel.

Lane stiffened. His entire body was so tight, Walker worried Lane would strain a muscle. Walker also feared his heart wouldn't recover from Lane's obvious disgust. He swore he could feel the hatred bleeding from Lane's pores. He walked away rubbing his chest. This wasn't how he wanted to spend what was left of his life. He had to find a way to get back to what they'd been before Orlando.

Mason stepped into his path, forcing Walker back on task. They were near to being the same age. Walker spent a moment marveling at how much younger Mason looked than him. Life had obviously been good to Mason. His auburn hair and green eyes always turned heads. It didn't hurt that he had the perfect number of freckles to sell people on his innocence. That is, until they got a look at his cut body. That was made for sin.

Mason's eyes swam with concern. "Hey."

"Hey." The word dragged out as Walker scrambled to understand Mason's mood.

"The place has been crazy busy tonight. This is the first chance I've gotten to ask how you're feeling."

"Oh." Walker blinked. Mason had obviously been told. He wondered if Lane had. Surely not, but then again, he was pretty pissed. "I'm all right. Tired, but..." Walker shrugged. He was uncomfortable.

Mason nodded, as if it was understandable for Walker to be exhausted. "I was surprised to see you come in tonight." He motioned toward his face. "Your eyes are black."

"Yeah," Walker said with a shrug. "I guess that's just part of it. Since I wasn't feeling terrible..." that was a lie "... and Trace needed help, I figured I'd lend a hand."

"That's good. I'm glad to see you. Hopefully, you'll—"

"Mason. People are still loitering in the parking lot. Can you take care of that?"

Walker fought the urge to look Lane's way. It

was the first time he'd heard the man's voice in two weeks. He'd never missed someone so badly. It didn't help that all the things he'd been prepared to face hadn't been as easy as he hoped. Sometimes, he wasn't as strong as he'd like.

Mason flashed him an apologetic smile over the interruption. He patted Walker's shoulder and headed for the door. Intimidation was what Trace paid Mason to do. It was time for him to get back to work. Walker was grateful. He couldn't handle Mason's pity. That had been the biggest reason for his silence. He hadn't wanted everyone to look at him exactly the way Mason looked at him.

Walker spent the next hour watching Lane for another opening. The moment Lane sat on the loveseat with his laptop in the VIP lounge, Walker filled the other half before someone stole his spot. Lane shifted as if to stand. Summer and Mason filled the other chairs, leaving Lane no other choice but to stay next to Walker. Lane's jaw flexed in his irritation. Walker bit back a smile. He had Lane trapped now.

"What's everyone's plans for the rest of the weekend?"

Walker loved how Dillion pulled up a seat in the VIP lounge alongside the employees like the place hadn't closed two hours earlier. It seemed money and a twink baby face truly bought everything because no one called him on it. Walker was too tired and sick to care.

Summer kicked her feet up onto the table and slid lower in her seat. "I need to snag a couple hours of sleep before I'm due to be at my aunt's for a family barbecue."

"That sounds nice," Lane said, sounding distracted as he openly ignored Walker's every attempt to get the boy to look his way. He'd intentionally sat too close to Lane on the loveseat, bumped his knee several times, and kept staring at him. Nothing. Lane kept his gaze locked firmly on his laptop. His eyes didn't budge. It was obvious he wasn't reading anything. He was simply ignoring Walker.

Summer barked out a forced laugh. "You'd think. My parents are great, but the rest of the fam are nothing but a bunch of racist, homophobic bastards. So I can't take Zoe, for obvious reasons, which means she's pissed and accusing me of hiding her."

"Sounds like she has a point," Walker said, pointing out the flaw in her argument.

Summer ignored him. "Hey, Lane, you're straight and single," Summer said, as if just remembering those things. "Do you want to come to a family cookout with me tomorrow and pretend to be my man? I'll owe you big time."

Lane didn't look up from his laptop. "Sure. I've got nothing else."

To anyone else, Lane probably sounded like he'd lost track in the middle of his sentence and not finished. Walker knew Lane had said exactly what he meant. He didn't feel like he had anything else. Fuck. Walker hated this. He hadn't intended to cut Lane so deeply. They just couldn't be together. It wouldn't be fair.

Lane snapped the lid closed on his laptop and finished grinding Walker's heart to dust as he stood to leave. "By the way, I'm not straight. I'm demisexual. That's why I'm single. No one cares about me like I care about them, so I don't bother. Text me the details. I've got to run." He tucked the laptop beneath his arm. "Everyone, be careful going home."

A round of goodbyes followed Lane out the door. Walker tried not to watch him go. Instead, he stretched out one leg and stared at his shoe—like something interesting went on down there. In truth, he tried not to scream and break shit. Every time he thought matters couldn't get worse, he learned another tidbit about Lane that made him guiltier. He'd purposely gotten close to Lane. Walker had known every step of the way that he shouldn't. He'd been self-aware through every heated glance and open flirt he'd sent Lane's way. Walker had known there was no hope for a future between them. Yet he hadn't stopped.

"I wonder what's going on with Lane," Summer mused aloud.

Dillion snorted, sounding like the judgmental twat he was. "I like high Lane better. He was fun. Clean Lane is uptight. He never flirts with me anymore. I always knew he wasn't serious, but damn. He's boring now. It's almost like he hates me."

Walker rubbed his temples. That was probably his fault.

Mason chimed in, "I disagree. It's not the sobriety. This is new. Before he left for vacation, he had me laughing so hard one night, I literally almost peed myself. I think something else is going on with him." He smiled in the wicked way Mason was best at. "I have to say, though, the demisexual news is fucking with me a little. Never really thought I had a shot before now."

"Agreed," Dillion said with a wink. "I like a challenge."

Walker rubbed his temples again.

"Well, I'm going to ask," Mason said, pushing to his feet and going after Lane.

All Walker could do was watch it happen in silent rage.

"Maybe Trace chastised him for fraternization or something," Summer offered, keeping the conversation moving. "That would explain why he hasn't really been talking to anyone."

Dillion shook his head. "That doesn't sound like Trace." His light green gaze swung Walker's way. "That does sound like Walker, though. You're being awful quiet over there. Care to chime in?"

Walker stood. "It's not right to talk about a man when he's not here to defend himself. I have work to do."

As Walker walked away, he heard Dillion snort again. "That settles it. He definitely had something to do with it."

Walker's eyes fell closed. His shoulders felt like they weighed a ton. Dillion was righter than he could possibly know, and Walker had no idea how to fix it.

***

Everything hurt. Bone deep, Lane ached.

With Walker nearby, Lane thought the first pangs were emotional. The closer he got to the car, the more he realized the pains were physical too. He hadn't seen his gorgeous giant since they'd gotten back from Orlando. Walker looked tired. The idea made Lane's chest hurt. He hated this. Missing Walker was like missing a limb. Lane made too big of a fool of himself their last night together. He couldn't forgive himself for making that stupid move. They'd been friends. In fact, Walker was the only real friend Lane had. Now, he had no one.

Trace and Hunter were in California, visiting Trace's family. Not that it mattered. He didn't feel like he could talk to Trace about this. Lane was on his own in his misery.

A wave of nausea overwhelmed Lane, heralding the oncoming invisible knives that nearly took him to his knees. Fuck. He usually had some warning before a flare-up. Unfortunately, Lane had spent so much time obsessing over Walker's presence, he hadn't been paying attention to his body. It was no wonder he was ten times more emotional over Walker showing up at the club. There was only so much he could handle at one time.

Mason ran him down before he made his escape.

"Lane. Hold up. You know I can't let you walk out alone. I'd lose my job."

Lane kept his gaze locked on his feet and prayed he wouldn't puke. The stabbing sensations were that intense. "It'll be our secret," Lane gasped out, sounding every bit as bad as he feared.

"Whoa," Mason said, grabbing his arm. "Are you okay?"

A whimper escaped Lane. Even the light pressure of Mason's touch was too intense. He fought the darkness closing around the edges of his vision.

Mason immediately released him. "Holy shit. Sorry. I guess I don't know my strength."

Lane swiped his hand through the air, waving off the apology. He finally managed to meet Mason's stare. The concern etched in Mason's face made Lane feel like shit. He genuinely liked the sexy bouncer. It wasn't Mason's fault Lane was a mess. "It's not you. Sorry." He rubbed his forehead, trying to think through the cloud. "I've been so busy, I forgot a few doses of my meds. This will pass. Don't worry over me." That wasn't exactly true. Lane had purposely missed those doses. The sad truth was he was a recovering addict. Taking pain killers chafed. Each time he swallowed one of those pills, Lane was scared shitless he'd be back in rehab, disappointing everyone. Lane's throat swelled. He was so fucking tired of life. It was terrifying how much he didn't want to go on.

"Let me drive you home."

Lane shook his head and managed a smile he didn't feel. "I'm good. It's not that far."

Mason was sweet. His expression grew more worried by the second. "Can I still walk you to your car? Make me feel a little useful."

At Mason's playful tone, Lane tried harder to hide how quickly he was fading. "Of course, but for the record, I happen to think you're very useful." He headed for his Jeep.

Mason fell into step beside him. "Really? Do tell. I love talking about me."

Lane snorted. It was nice to have a distraction. "You can reach high things and carry heavy boxes."

A sexy-sounding chuckle floated through the air. "You make me sound like I'm your houseboy. Not that I'm complaining," Mason tacked on before Lane could apologize. "I happen to think I'd make one hell of a houseboy. I'm up for any task you need performed. Any task." Mason's voice dripped with sex, leaving no doubt to his meaning.

Lane shook his head, incapable of hiding his

disbelief. "You're a mess. Does anyone ever take you up on that? Don't answer that," Lane quickly added. "I'm sure everyone does."

Mason winced. "Ouch. From houseboy to whore."

Lane sucked in a breath. He was winning all over the place tonight. "Sorry. I didn't mean it that way. I just meant, you're gorgeous and obviously popular."

Mason's sexy chuckle had Lane trailing off. "I'm just fucking with you. This job has its perks—like meeting someone new every night, but you might be surprised. I kind of like the idea of going home to the same person every night."

"But you don't intend to," Lane surmised.

"Nope."

Mason's shamelessness had Lane shaking his head and laughing. Life was so easy for some people. He wasn't jealous. Not really, but sometimes he wondered what it must be like to be so free. "Well, here's my Jeep," Lane said as they reached his door.

The way Mason shifted from foot to foot, shoving his hands in his pockets while glancing around let Lane know he wasn't ready to let Lane go before saying whatever had him chasing Lane outside to begin with. Lane stood still and waited.

He hoped Mason got there soon because his head pounded to the point of making his vision blur. He finally focused on Lane, looking resolute. "What happened between Walker and you?"

The air left Lane's lungs like he'd been punched in the chest. He'd never expected to be in this position. Lane scrambled to think of what to say. He couldn't be honest.

Before he managed a lie, Mason swiped his hand through the air. "You don't have to answer that. It's not any of my business. The thing is, life is short, you know? You don't want to end up with regrets."

Mason had no idea. All Lane had was regrets. There was no area of his life where he could look and not see someplace he'd gone wrong. It was almost as if he didn't know how to do anything right. Maybe leaving Walker alone was the first time he'd done what was best. Deep down, Lane knew he was a waste of time, and probably wouldn't make it much longer. He wouldn't steal more from Walker. Lane swallowed past the pain. "I appreciate your concern. Walker deserves more friends like you."

His response had Mason looking more offended than when Lane implied he was a whore. "I'm your friend too."

Lane smiled and nodded, the way he always did,

even though he knew he was really alone. "Of course."

Mason brightened and Lane swallowed the bitterness. "We should go out sometime. Seriously. Like a date."

"Sounds great." Lane didn't mean a word. Tonight had made some decisions for him. The biggest one was that he was through with this scene. When he'd gotten home from Orlando, he'd talked himself into not quitting Incubus. Trace needed him. Now he knew the truth. No one needed him. Not really. He'd turn in his notice to Trace and stay long enough to find a replacement, but he was done. Lane had only stayed on as a way to repay Trace for all he'd done—putting Lane through rehab and financing his startup. The thing was, Lane was beginning to feel like the price was too high. He couldn't keep paying with his soul. There was a lot he was pretty sure he couldn't do any longer. Seeing Walker was at the top of that list.

Dillion clung to the shadows, waiting until Lane pulled from the lot before heading to his car. He wanted to be angry. All Dillion knew how to do any longer was how to hurt. Hell would freeze before he showed it. With his head held high, he made a beeline for his car. Acting skills and bravery aside, Dillion would rather not catch Mason's attention. He almost made it. His hand was on the door. Fingers slipped down his spine. Dillion's eyes fell closed.

"I had a dream about you last night."

Dillion didn't turn. Not yet. He knew there was no way Mason wouldn't see the devastation if he turned now.

"You were wearing a tiny skirt that stopped right below your perfect ass. Underneath, you had on a white lace thong. Thigh-high stockings. A crop top that stopped right below your hardened nipples. Do you think you could find that outfit to wear for me?"

Fuck him. Dillion would wear that in a heartbeat. But not for Mason. Not anymore. He slowly turned, wearing his sweetest of smiles. "I think I'll pass. Your bed is a little too crowded for me."

Mason took a step closer. His fingers found a lock of Dillion's hair. His gaze stayed locked on where he toyed with Dillion's short curls. "You're so soft—like a peach. My bed is empty at the moment." His gaze dropped to Dillion's. Dillion's throat swelled at the heat in his stare. Mason shifted even closer. "I can still picture you in that tiny skirt. You were bent over my lap, taking the punishment you deserve." Dillion's body responded without his permission. He could almost feel the sting of Mason's palm. "After you begged, I had my way with your hot, tight boy pussy."

Dillion hated him. He really did. Mason knew what to say to get under his skin. Knew the exact words that would light a fire in Dillion's blood. But pleasure with Mason was fleeting. The pain he spread around like wildfire, scarred. Dillion flattened his palm against Mason's chest. For a moment, his traitorous fingers caressed Mason's hard muscles before he pushed him away. "You're taking your shot with Lane, remember? I'm no one's second choice." In truth, it was more likely Dillion was Mason's final choice. Incubus had closed without Mason finding a bed partner for the night. Dillion was there. He was easy. Mason would settle for him. Dillion didn't want to be the consolation prize.

Mason shrugged. "Lane isn't interested in me. You know that." He moved closer, ignoring Dillion's attempt at keeping him held away. "But you didn't hesitate to jump at your chance the moment you heard he didn't care about a person's gender."

Mason's mouth lifted in one corner. "That matters a lot to someone like you."

That one hurt. Dillion didn't want to play anymore. He turned away, intent on opening his door. Before he could get away, Dillion found himself hauled back against Mason's chest. He didn't fight. Instead, he went limp. The streetlight above shined on Dillion's car. He could see his reflection in the driver's side window. As he looked on, Mason pressed his lips to the shell of Dillion's ear. He looked so tiny in Mason's hold. Dillion felt even smaller on the inside. Loving someone wasn't supposed to feel this way. That much he knew.

"I'm sorry, sweets. You know I think you're perfect."

Dillion didn't respond. He couldn't. His voice would crack if he spoke that lie, and he'd let Mason steal too much of him already.

Mason's hand ran down his body, stroking Dillion like a cat. "Come home with me, angel. I'll make it better."

Dillion couldn't tear his gaze away from his reflection, especially his eyes. They looked exactly how he felt on the inside—dead. That was what loving Mason was like. Nothing would ever change.

FOUR

WALKER: *Do you ever intend to talk to me again?*

Walker: *I don't know how to fix things if you won't talk to me.*

Walker: *At least tell me if you made it home okay?*

Walker: *If I don't hear from you in the next ten minutes, I'm coming to find you. You're not allowed to be dead in a ditch somewhere.*

Walker: *Time's up. If you don't want to see me, you'd better speak now.*

Walker: *On my way.*

LANE'S APARTMENT WAS DARK, AND HIS JEEP WAS

parked in its usual spot. Still, something felt off. No matter how angry Lane might be, Walker couldn't imagine the man deliberately forcing Walker to drive over to check on him. He'd want Walker to stay away. Walker stared at Lane's door and chewed his bottom lip. It was possible Lane slept peacefully inside. The dread in Walker's gut said something else. He swore he could feel the wrongness in the air.

With a growl, he threw open his truck door and made a beeline for the door. Determination carried him every step. He knocked. No one answered. Not a single sound stirred. Walker used his spare key to get in. He couldn't leave without knowing. A million thoughts raced through his mind. Every horror possible flitted across his brain in a matter of seconds. His heart raced and every breath he took came harder than the last until he felt like he sucked air through a straw. Walker could live with Lane's anger. He couldn't live without him.

The living room was dark. Only a light spilling from the hallway showed the room was empty.

Walker closed the door behind him. "Lane? Are you here?"

"Fucking what?" The growled question came down the hall. It sounded slurred, bringing one of Walker's fears to the forefront. Lane was using again.

The instant rage carried him down the hall. He didn't bother looking in the darkened kitchen or the two empty bedrooms before storming into Lane's room. The light was on. Lane was curled into a ball. Wearing nothing more than workout shorts and a hoodie, Lane's eyes shone bright with pain and rage. He stared at Walker in silence. A muscle in his jaw worked where he obviously ground his teeth against the torture. Walker's throat swelled. His head pounded. He felt really bad and should've stayed home tonight. Now he was glad he hadn't. Otherwise, he might not have checked on Lane and Lane would be here suffering alone.

Walker crossed the room and sat on the edge of the bed. "Is there anything that doesn't hurt?"

Lane squeezed his eyes closed as if a wave of agony washed over him. He lightly rocked himself as if trying desperately to get any comfort through the pain. "My hands," he finally gasped out.

Walker would take it. Any place he could touch worked for him. He took one of Lane's hands between his and rubbed. Walker massaged the pressure points, hoping to bring him any relief he could. For the first time, Walker wondered if Trace and he had made a mistake by convincing Lane to get clean. When Lane had tried to explain he lived in misery, Walker hadn't understood. Not really. At the time, in his ignorance, he'd thought he got it. He'd thought he understood pain. Watching Lane now, Walker realized he hadn't known anything. No one should be forced to live like this. He didn't know how there could be such a horrible condition as this and there be no real treatment. Walker was learning some things about health lately. Mostly, that it was more common than he ever dreamed for there to be nothing anyone could do. People weren't always fixed by medicine. Sometimes, people just suffered.

His eyes burned. Hating himself was becoming a regular state for Walker. "I'm so sorry, baby."

"Stop," Lane gasped. "I hurt too bad right now to pander to your feelings." Even though he knew Lane was only being honest because he was in agony and not guarding his words, Walker was oddly relieved to have Lane's anger. "You don't have to sit by me through this. In fact, I'd prefer if you didn't, so get off the cross and go home."

Ouch. That one hit a little close to home. Who was he making feel better by coming here? Lane or himself? He stroked Lane's hand one more time. "Okay, babe. I get it. Please call me if you think you need to go to the hospital." Without thought, Walker leaned in and kissed Lane's cheek. It seemed the natural thing to do. Except Lane turned his head at the last second and their lips met instead. Walker froze. He didn't pull away. Lane's lips parted beneath his before sweetly closing on Walker's bottom lip. From there, Lane's lips moved to the corner of Walker's mouth. Another soft kiss brushed his skin. His heart skipped a beat. Walker shot upright. An apology rose in his throat. The room spun and darkened around the edges.

"I'm." The single word left his lips sounding breathless and then there was nothing.

THERE WAS NOTHING FAMILIAR ABOUT THE OFF-white room. Walker shook off the last wisps of sleep and looked around. There was no mistaking he was in the hospital. His bed kept making that god-awful noise where it released air and pumped back up again. His gaze landed on Lane first. He was curled up on a small couch in the corner. The gray hoodie he'd been wearing when Walker went to see him still covered his head. Even in his sleep, Lane looked miserable.

"He's having a really bad flare-up. Like, worse than he's had in a long time," Trace said, dragging

Walker's gaze to the chair beside the bed where Trace sat. Trace should've been the first person he spotted. He was closer, but Lane was his heart. Sometimes, Walker couldn't see anyone else.

Walker scrubbed at his face, knocking the oxygen loose he hadn't known he wore. He took a better look at himself. There was an IV in his hand and his arm had a huge bruise forming. His head pounded, and he didn't feel so great. But Lane didn't look good, and that mattered more. "Why didn't you send him home or to the ER?"

Trace had dark circles under his eyes and looked like he might keel over at any time. He snorted at Walker's question. "You passed out in his bedroom floor, forcing him to call 911. There was no sending him away. Don't worry. He took a mega dose of prescriptions. He should be out for a while."

The tension bled from Walker's shoulders. "How much does he know?"

Trace held his stare. "Again, you passed out in his bedroom floor, forcing him to call 911. He knows everything."

Walker's eyes burned. Something about Lane knowing the truth made things realer than ever before. "You know I didn't want that."

"Why?" The croaked question had Walker's

gaze shooting to Lane. His eyes were open, and his pain-filled gaze was locked on Walker. "Why didn't you want me to know?"

"You should go home and rest."

Lane sat up, obviously set on powering through. "Don't worry about me. Answer the question."

Trace stood. "I'm going to step out and call Hunter." He made a beeline for the door like he was running for his life.

Walker understood. If he wasn't hooked up to an IV pole and thought his legs would work properly, he might run too. There was no avoiding this any longer. "You don't need my problems on top of yours."

Lane ran his tongue over his teeth, making Walker wonder what hateful words he swallowed. He visibly took a breath before responding. "So we're not friends. Is that what you're saying?"

That wasn't what he was saying, but he also wanted to scream they weren't friends. They were more and Lane fucking knew it. Unfortunately, that desire locked his thoughts too long.

Lane looked away and nodded. "I guess I'll go home, then. Sorry to have wasted so much of your time."

"Look at me."

Lane shook his head and kept his face averted. With the hood up on his hoodie, Walker couldn't see his expression. Lane stood. With his head down, he headed for the door.

Fear shot through Walker. Lane was in pain, mentally and physically. He might do anything when he got like this. "Lane." Lane hesitated with his hand on the doorknob, but he didn't look back. Walker scrambled to think of something to say. It was harder than usual with a brain tumor pressing on his gray matter. In his rush to make things right, he said the first dumbass thing that popped in his head. "Don't do anything stupid."

Lane finally looked his way. His eyes were bloodshot and red-rimmed. He looked like he'd been crying, but his eyes were also dead—like Walker had finally killed something inside him. "You've pretended to care long enough, don't you think?" Without waiting for a response, Lane slipped away before Walker absorbed the blow. Walker stared at the spot where Lane last stood. Maybe, if he lived, he'd find a way to fix things with Lane. If he didn't, it was possible those would be last words he ever heard from Lane. This would be Lane's last memory of them. Maybe it was for the best, or maybe he'd just lost the only thing that had kept him clinging to life. Either way, Walker lost.

LANE COULDN'T THINK. HE COULDN'T BREATHE. Walker had a brain tumor. He'd started chemo and radiation treatment two days ago. The trip he'd taken with Lane had been like a goodbye, according to Trace. Walker didn't expect to make it and he'd never had any intention of telling Lane. According to the doctor, Walker had passed out due to a combination of dehydration and a bad blood count. Apparently, chemo was kicking his ass, yet he'd still filled in for Trey and come to check on Lane. He should be in bed, resting. Lane should be taking care of him. The fact that they—apparently—weren't really friends didn't factor. But Lane couldn't make Walker want him around. The knowledge that he didn't cut Lane deeper than he'd ever imagined.

Lane was in so much pain, his knees didn't want to keep him moving. He'd powered through before. Lane would again. The thing was, he really didn't want to anymore. At the moment, he couldn't remember why he'd been fighting for so long. It seemed kind of pointless, to be honest. He was unnecessary to the world. His dad and Trace had each other. Walker didn't want or need him. Lane had nothing but the endless pain and Walker's obvious belief Lane would give in to the drugs or give up. Maybe he would. He hadn't decided which yet.

"Lane?"

Lane's head jerked up at the sound of his name. He'd almost made it to the door. Dillion headed in his direction. Lane swallowed the hurt. It seemed he'd almost left in time to miss Dillion racing to Walker's side. It appeared everyone had known about Walker's health but Lane. He wanted to lash out. Dillion couldn't love Walker the way Lane did. It wasn't fair for the guy to be massively rich, sexy, famous, and have Walker. Lane felt smaller by the second.

"Hey, Dillion."

Dillion closed the distance between them. There was a line between his eyebrows as if he was worried. "Are you okay?"

Lane nodded. It was a sharp and jerky motion, but he managed. "Just headed home." The words tailed off as he looked toward the parking lot. He'd ridden in the ambulance with Walker. Lane had no fucking clue how he was getting home.

"You don't look so good. Can I help?"

Lane's gaze swung back Dillion's way. He was so adorable. Tiny with short dark curls. He looked young—like super young. Lane had never thought about Dillion's age. He was obviously over eighteen or he wouldn't be allowed in Incubus, but damned if —in the light of day—Dillion didn't look fourteen. Lane never would've thought Dillion would've been Walker's type, especially since it hadn't been that long ago that Walker threatened to ban Dillion over Mason. But it seemed Lane didn't know shit about Walker or Dillion.

"I was just about to call a cab, I guess."

The concern in Dillion's stare grew. "You don't have to do that. I can take you home."

Lane wished he could run away. Instead, he shook his head. "I don't want to slow you down. Go visit with Walker. I can get home on my own."

The line between Dillion's eyes deepened. "Walker? Is Walker here? I just had lunch with my dad. He's the chief of staff here. But Walker's here? What happened?"

For a long minute, Lane stared at Dillion, trying to make his words make sense. He wasn't here for Walker. Jealousy was a bitter pill, it seemed. "Yeah," Lane finally said, trying to make his brain work. "Sorry. I'm heavily medicated right now. Fibro flare-

57

up. Your dad works here? That's..." He didn't know. Everything hurt too badly. His entire body had invisible knives carving away while his heart was like tiny shards of glass—shattered and cutting away at everything.

Dillion's face cleared. His light green gaze swept Lane's body, leaving Lane confused. Dillion motioned toward the doors they were currently blocking. "Come on. I have nothing but free time. Let me take you home."

Lane shook his head again, incapable of accepting the tiniest bit of help. "I don't want to put you out."

To his surprise, a bright smile lit Dillion's face. His innocence turned to wicked in an instant. He nudged Lane toward the door. "I put out all on my own. No one needs to twist my arm."

Lane allowed himself to be maneuvered, but curiosity kicked his ass. "How old are you anyhow?" he asked, keeping his gaze locked on Dillion as they hit the sidewalk.

Dillion's eyes flashed with humor. "I just have one of those faces." It was a non-answer if Lane had ever heard one.

They didn't have to walk far. It seemed being the son of the chief of staff had its perks. A good parking spot was one. The black and white Bugatti Veyron was probably due to Dillion's acting career. Aspen was filled with celebrities. He'd seen one or two people gush over Dillion, who'd grown up in front of the world on the big screen. He'd been one of the main characters in a series of huge blockbusters. While Lane doubted any of Dillion's life was private, Lane hadn't noticed his stardom keeping him from living a normal life. Three point four-million-dollar car aside, of course.

Lane gave Dillion his address and tried not to touch anything. They rode in companionable silence. Despite his pain, Lane found himself eyeing Dillion on the sly. He hadn't known Walker was in the hospital. Dillion also hadn't rushed to Walker's side or seemed overly concerned. His hands were pretty. It was such an odd thought to have, but Lane couldn't stop his mind from going there. Dillion had small, feminine hands. He wore a delicate-looking gold band on his middle finger. His nails were painted clear. Lane couldn't look away. His tanned skin with the gold against it fascinated Lane for reasons he couldn't explain. He didn't hurt as badly with his focus locked on Dillion's hands. Lane didn't realize he was home until Dillion spoke.

"How did I not know you own a weed store? That's so deliciously you."

Lane smiled. It felt genuine for the first time in at least a week. "I'm not sure we've ever talked about anything personal. The place hasn't been open long, and I have employees running it most of the time. My apartment is in the back."

Dillion nodded toward the small lane beside the store. "Will that take me to your door?"

"Yeah. There's a small parking area back there."

"Cool," Dillion said, backing from his parking spot and maneuvering down the lane.

A smile tugged at Lane's lips. "I could've walked."

"I don't doubt it, but then you wouldn't have felt obligated to invite me in."

Lane's smile grew. He shook his head. He liked Dillion a little more by the second. He found himself staring at Dillion as Dillion backed his car into the space next to Lane's Jeep. Walker's truck was gone. Lane wondered how he'd pulled that off. He couldn't think about Walker anymore. "Would you like to come in?"

Dillion's gaze slid his way. Lane marveled over how truly beautiful he was. For the first time, he realized Dillion wore a hint of makeup. "I'd love to.

Thanks for thinking of me," Dillion said with a chuckle as he opened his door.

Lane's smile slipped away on a gasp of pain as he put weight on his legs again. He kept his head down as he dug his keys out on the way to the door. When he glanced up, he caught Dillion eyeing him.

Dillion didn't play coy. "What hurts the most?"

Lane fucking hated this. He felt lacking and broken next to Dillion's flawless existence. Lane took stock. "My head."

Dillion nodded but waited until they were inside to strike. "First off, you need an edible. Then you should strip."

In the center of his living room, while staring at a man he never expected to be under his roof, Lane blanked. "I'm sorry."

Dillion's expression said he wouldn't be disobeyed. "You know as well as I do that marijuana is one of the best treatments for Fibro. It's much safer than the poison they put in painkillers. So, edible first. Just something small like a gummie or a sucker. Then strip."

"Um." Lane shifted from foot to foot. "Why?" The word dragged out, sounding every bit as confused as Lane was.

Dillion shrugged. "You should trust me. If you'd

like, you can leave on your shorts, but the hoodie and shirt have to go." Dillion winked. "You can lose the shorts too, if you'd like." Lane didn't move. Dillion sighed. He plucked the keys from Lane's hand and tossed them on the coffee table. Since he hadn't been living there long and things were still a mess, there were boxes of inventory in his living room. Dillion didn't ask permission. He simply dove in, found the suckers, ripped one open, and shoved it in Lane's mouth. Lane stood, frozen, and unable to fight the miniature hurricane known as Dillion while Dillion worked the hoodie and t-shirt off Lane's body. He also touched Lane a lot more than was strictly necessary for the job.

His fingers swiped down Lane's torso. "Face down on the couch."

Lane didn't know how to disobey. He moved to his cushy microfiber couch and stretched out on his stomach. Dillion sat next to his hip and massaged his neck. With the sucker in his cheek and his face turned Dillion's way, Lane tried not to think. He'd avoided edibles since leaving rehab for fear of backsliding, but he knew Dillion was right. For medicinal purposes, it was the best treatment. Mostly, he just hadn't wanted Walker to think of him as a failure. He would never touch the hard stuff again. That much he knew. He didn't want to go back to being that person. But he also couldn't continue struggling against this pain without relief. Between learning Walker never thought of him as a friend and hurting nonstop, he was slipping into a dark place he wouldn't survive. He didn't know why Dillion was being so nice, but goddamn. His touch was amazing. Dillion kept digging his fingers into the perfect pressure point, one Lane hadn't realized existed. The headache crushing his brain eased a little more by the second. The tension drained from his muscles.

"Damn. That feels good." Even to his ears, Lane sounded relaxed.

When Dillion responded, he kept his voice pitched low, as if trying to soothe Lane into sleep. "Back when I was on set eighteen hours a day, I was either training for the next scene or filming the next scene. I had to always be perfect, no matter how much my muscles screamed in protest. Countless times, I powered through injuries to get the job done. The only relief I got was from this masseuse. He taught me which pressure points relieved different pains. Those lessons have had their perks—like now."

Lane's head was a little fuzzy. It was possible he shouldn't have accepted the sucker on top of his pain meds. "If I didn't know better, I'd think you were coming on to me." Lane wished he hadn't said that, but his tongue didn't want to obey good sense.

Dillion slid to his knees next to Lane's head. His light green gaze looked serious and understanding. Lane's throat swelled at the sight. "If you weren't in love with Walker, I'd admit that I am coming on to you, but I know you don't want me." A sad smile touched Dillion's lips. "Maybe that's exactly why I'm here. I could do anything right now and you still wouldn't want me. We're both pretty safe."

Lane blinked, fighting the stinging behind his eyes. He got tired of wishing he was someone else. Someone who'd reach for Dillion and forget Walker. "Walker doesn't love me back, so it doesn't matter." In this moment, Lane didn't care if Dillion saw his heart.

Dillion set his arm on the couch. With his hand resting on Lane's back and his chin on his arm, Dillion held Lane's stare. His face was so close, Lane could feel each exhaled breath across his skin. "He's a fool then." Dillion took the sucker from Lane's mouth and set it on the wrapper he'd left on the table before resuming his earlier pose. His fingertips lightly stroked Lane's back, threatening to put him to sleep. "Close your eyes, sweetie. I'll take care of you."

Lane's eyes slipped closed. He relaxed a little more by the second with Dillion's breath fanning his face and his fingers luring him under.

Dillion's voice soothed his soul. "Maybe one day, when you're feeling better, I'll tell you what it's like to be me. You're not alone. The person I love the most doesn't want me either."

Lane hated to think Dillion's life was anything but perfect. Right now, he couldn't stay awake to tell him as much. Beneath Dillion's touch, everything slipped away.

FIVE

WALKER: *Have you seen Lane? I'm at his apartment, but he's not here.*

Trace: *He's here at Incubus, ordering stock. Hurry if you want to catch him before he leaves.*

Walker: *On my way.*

———

THERE WAS ONLY ONE CAR IN THE LOT AT Incubus, Trace's Range Rover. Walker rushed to the door, expecting he'd already missed seeing Lane. His heart slowed at the first sight of Lane bent over a clipboard. Trace caught sight of him first. He took the clipboard from Lane and openly ran for the hills. Lane's head turned following

Trace's escape. Then he turned. Their gazes met. Walker almost missed a step, but his feet didn't stop moving.

Lane openly eyed Walker's stocking cap as Walker crossed the room. "Are you losing your hair already?"

Walker pulled off the cap, showing off his bald head before pulling the cap back on. "A little, but I went ahead and shaved it. If they manage to shrink the tumor, they'll shave my hair for surgery, so I might as well get used to it."

Lane nodded. He wouldn't meet Walker's stare and it hurt Walker's chest. Walker had done that. He'd hurt the man he loved with his secrets and silence. Even though Walker didn't know how to fix things, he knew staying away wasn't the answer. "So, I was wondering if you'd like to go to lunch?" He needed to apologize. They needed to talk. Walker couldn't live with the silence or guilt.

"Um." His gaze focused on something over Walker's shoulder. "I already have plans."

"Oh."

"Are you ready, Lane?"

Walker's eyes fell closed at the sound of Dillion's voice behind him. He'd recognize that over-privileged tone anywhere. When his eyes reopened,

Walker found Lane watching him. Walker pasted on a fake smile. "That's cool. Some other time, I guess."

Lane's gaze moved between Dillion and him. His expression gave nothing away. "We could go to dinner, if you'd like?"

"Two dates in one day? Are you sure you can handle it?" Even though Walker tried for a joking tone, he failed miserably. Biting sarcasm tinged every word. Even he cringed against it.

Lane's features hardened. Walker swore he felt Lane's heart slam closed against him. Lane tried stepping around him without saying goodbye. Walker snagged his arm before he could get away. Lane's gaze dropped to where Walker held him. His cold gaze lifted. Hatred bled from his stare and nearly blasted Walker from his feet.

"I'm sorry." The apology tumbled from Walker's lips. He didn't know how to stop fucking up with Lane, but he needed to start somewhere. "There's a lot I need to say. Whenever you have time for me, okay?"

Lane gave him a jerky nod and pulled away. As Walker looked on in helpless silence, Lane crossed the room, going to Dillion. He wanted to scream and break shit. Unfortunately, he'd already broken the most important piece of his life. He rubbed his chest.

Everything hurt. Every time he thought about how far Lane had put himself out there with Walker, only to have Walker stab him through the heart, he felt sick all over again. Walker imagined it felt a lot like this, watching Lane leave with someone else. Someone better. He took a breath. Lane gave him exactly what he deserved. Walker would wait until tonight. Whatever it took.

"Do you want to talk about it?"

Walker's gaze moved Trace's way. Trace was good at making himself scarce while still managing to witness Walker's every downfall. Trace also had a way of always looking like he understood, even though Walker was certain no one could. He shrugged. "I'm not sure there's anything to say. I fucked up."

Trace didn't spare his feelings. "Yeah. You did. But you know it, so now you can fix it."

Walker moved to join Trace on the loveseat. He missed their late nights together, talking or just working in companionable silence. Life had been simple once. "It's not fair for me to have shown up here. He's still better off without me. If I die…"

"If you die, it'll hurt Lane every bit as much no matter what you do." Trace sounded sure and stern. "You can't protect anyone from this."

"I love him." The words came so easily. They came from Walker's heart.

Trace smiled. "I know. I guess you'd better start fighting then."

"Is that even possible now? I don't know how to compete against a millionaire baby-faced actor in a Bugatti."

A snort of laughter escaped Trace. Blue eyes filled with humor swung Walker's way. "As much as I never thought I'd be saying this about Lane, he doesn't care about money. That store of his is raking in the dough. I know because he keeps trying to pay me back double what I gave him for the startup. Yet he still chooses to live in that tiny apartment in back. He bought a used Jeep, for Christ's sake. As far as I know, that's the only thing he's bought for himself in the past year. Above all else, though, he loves you too. You don't have to win him from Dillion. He's already yours. But you do owe him a huge apology for hiding this from him," Trace said, motioning toward Walker's head. If only Trace knew. Walker owed Lane an apology for so much more than his silence. He wasn't sure he could be forgiven.

"I'll figure something out." Walker wasn't sure if it was true, but he would try. There was no low he wouldn't stoop to when it came to Lane. Even if it meant taking out Dillion's knees.

WALKER WAS SITTING IN HIS DRIVEWAY. A nervous flutter began in Lane's gut at the first sight of the man's giant truck parked outside Lane's door. Fear shot through him when he spotted Walker behind the wheel, leaned against the door with his eyes closed. Lane jumped from his Jeep before he'd finished rolling and circled the truck. When he eased the door open, hoping Walker wouldn't fall out, Walker shot up, blinking. He looked confused until he focused on Lane. His face softened.

"Hey. Sorry. I must've dozed off."

Lane bent at the waist and sucked air. His heartbeat pounded in his ears while he tried calming his racing heart. "You scared the hell out of me being all slumped over like that." Lane straightened. His fear turned to fury. "You should've just used the spare key and went inside. It's not good for you to be sitting out here all day."

Walker rubbed his eyes. He still looked lost and half asleep. "I'm sorry."

"Stop apologizing," Lane snapped. He took

another calming breath. His shoulders sagged. "Come on." He headed for the door, feeling like he weighed a ton. Lane couldn't handle the thought of anything happening to Walker. Damn it. He was barely clinging to sanity and sobriety as it was. With his keys in the door, Lane froze as Walker's arms encircled him—one arm around his waist and the other across Lane's throat, preventing him from getting away. He invaded Lane's space. His face burrowed in the crook of Lane's neck as his chest collided with Lane's back. Goosebumps rose on Lane's skin as Walker took a deep breath against the side of Lane's neck. "Please don't be mad anymore." Each word of Walker's plea brushed Lane's skin. "You're my best friend. I should've said that."

Lane's eyes burned. He dropped his chin to the forearm Walker had around his throat. Lane didn't know how to fight Walker. He didn't know if he wanted to do this anymore either. It hurt too much, being in love alone. "How could you choose to do this without me?" That was the gist of things. Walker had every intention of shutting him out. After everything, Lane didn't understand.

"How can I drag you through this?"

Lane turned in Walker's hold. Walker's arms fell away, but his hands lingered on Lane's hips and he didn't step back. "It's not dragging if I want to be there. That's who we are," Lane said, motioning between them. "Through everything life throws our way, we stick together. You're supposed to know that. You're supposed to know..."

Walker's gaze deepened. He looked as if he held his breath. "What am I supposed to know?" Walker asked when Lane didn't finish.

Lane spent a moment wondering if he was brave enough for this. Then he spent another wondering if he could live without Walker ever knowing. One was heavier than the other. There was no real choice. Lane felt how he felt, and it wasn't going away. "You're supposed to know that I love you." It came out sounding small, but it came out.

Walker took a step closer. Lane's back went against the door. There was nowhere for him to hide. The intensity in Walker's gaze took Lane's breath. "You're asking me to accept I might leave you behind."

"That was already true. I'm asking you to fight to stay... with me." There was this huge unknown between them. Lane wasn't sure he'd ever really known himself before Walker. But he was willing to do whatever it took, and he needed Walker to be the same. If that wasn't the way of things, it was better for Walker to say so now.

Walker touched Lane's hair—like he'd been fighting the urge. His gaze moved to where Lane's hair slipped through his fingers. "No more dates with Dillion."

"He's just a friend."

Walker's gaze slid back to his. "Before today, you could say the same of me."

Lane held Walker's stare. "You've never been just a friend."

Walker touched his forehead to Lane's. "You're the strongest person I know."

He didn't feel strong. Lane's insides shook in terror. He stood to lose everything—Walker. Himself. Everything he'd thought he knew. Lane's fingers found Walker's shirt. He held on. "Stop trying to think of a way to let me down easy and say what you mean."

Somehow, Walker managed to look even more intense up close. "I'm not sure you're ready for my thoughts."

Lane started to pull away. He was tired of playing games.

Walker refused to budge, keeping Lane trapped. "I'm scared." Lane froze. He'd never expected that confession. Walker wasn't finished. "What if I kiss you and you decide this isn't what you want?"

Lane didn't bother answering. Instead, he touched his lips to Walker's and backed away an inch. Walker seemed to hold his breath. Lane did it again. This time, he held still and waited. There was no way Walker couldn't feel how he shook. He'd never been more terrified. Walker shuffled closer. His fingers tightened on Lane's hips. Lane flattened his palms on Walker's chest and swept upward until his arms encircled Walker's neck. Walker's tongue lightly stroked Lane's top lip. Lane automatically opened, chasing him. His head fell back against the door as Walker went on the attack. Walker's tongue filled his mouth, stroking Lane's. Lane met him stroke for stroke. The kiss went from hot and heavy to over in an instant. Walker leaned away and shook his head. He looked pale.

Panic gripped Lane. He quickly unlocked the door. "Come on. Don't pass out on me again."

Walker's eyes opened. The sweet brown gaze that had found its way beneath Lane's skin focused on Lane. "I'm okay. You make the blood rush from my brain," he tacked on with a chuckle.

Lane smiled, even though he didn't feel it. Terror

still held his throat in its grip. "Still. Ease my mind and come sit down."

"Hold on," Walker said, holding tight to Lane's shirt so he couldn't get away. "I have something I need to say."

Lane's mind raced. Surely they'd said everything. "Okay."

Walker gave him a sharp nod. His chest expanded as if he took a deep breath for courage. "I love you. If you decide you can't do this, I'll understand, but I need you to know you're the only one for me."

A hint of a smile touched Lane's lips. "We've got this the way we do everything. Together." Lane believed in them. He knew Walker did too or Walker wouldn't be here. Maybe before today neither of them admitted it, but they were always meant to end up right here. They were a team. Lane wasn't sure even death could tear them apart.

As Lane led Walker to his bedroom, Walker couldn't look away. *You're supposed to know I love you.* Those words kept trailing through his mind, kicking over every belief he'd had about what was right. Walker had been certain he should let Lane go. Set him free from the horror Walker faced. Lane was right. It was too late even before he learned of his tumor. They were already in this together whether they were together or not.

Lane emptied his pockets onto the bedside table and toed off his shoes. Walker did the same without thought. It slowly penetrated his mind they were standing next to Lane's bed. Then Lane climbed in and Walker watched in confusion.

Lane patted the empty spot beside him. "You're supposed to be resting. Don't lie and say otherwise."

"I'm okay." Lane had literally just warned him not to lie. It was habit, telling everyone he was fine.

An adorable half smile crossed Lane's lips. "Let me take care of you."

"I should be taking care of you," Walker grumbled even as he did as told.

Lane rolled and Walker automatically rolled with him, making Lane into the little spoon he was. A content-sounding sigh escaped Lane. After a moment, Lane spoke haltingly. "I may be broken myself, but I can still take care of you through this. You may as well accept my babying with the minimum amount of grumbling."

Despite not wanting Lane to feel obligated,

Walker was relieved to not be alone. "We'll take care of each other." Walker kissed Lane's nape. Once his lips landed on Lane, he couldn't stop. He kissed Lane's shoulder and then his cheek. He pecked away at Lane like a starving chicken. The harder Lane laughed, the more Walker kissed him. Lane's open happiness did more than swell Walker's chest. It also had him turned on to the point of painful.

There was so much wrong with his timing. He was still weak from his chemo and hospital stint. Lane needed time to acclimate being with a man. While he did an amazing job of treating this new dynamic in his life as business as usual, Walker knew things weren't so cut and dry. There was nothing Walker loved better than knowing Lane had fallen in love with his soul rather than Walker's parts. Still, Walker didn't want to move too fast and scare him. Walker's dick didn't care about any of that. There was a middle ground, though. He felt sure Lane wouldn't balk at some mutual pleasure play.

Walker lightly nipped at Lane's earlobe. "So," he said, dragging out the word. "How do you feel about finishing that blow job you started in Florida?"

A horrified-sounding bark of laughter exploded from Lane. He snagged the pillow and covered his face, muffling the sound and hiding his blush. It was too late. Walker had already seen his reddened cheeks before he'd hidden. He tried stealing Lane's pillow. Lane wouldn't let him have it. Walker rolled to his knees and straddled Lane's hips after urging him into his back. Since Lane wouldn't uncover his face, Walker kissed Lane's stomach instead. He moved lower, kissing a path down Lane's body. Walker pushed Lane's shirt higher and kissed Lane's bare stomach. Lane's arms fell away from the pillow, but he didn't come out. A muffled moan sneaked out from beneath the pillow as Walker massaged Lane's cock through his clothes. Walker popped the button loose on Lane's jeans. He slid Lane's zipper down tooth by tooth while circling Lane's navel with his tongue.

"You're supposed to be resting." The admonishment came out sounding breathless even while muted by the pillow. Lane's erection told a different story from his mouth.

"I'm in bed," Walker reminded him.

Lane finally uncovered his face and stared down the line of his body at Walker. "I can't fucking believe you were awake. Do you have any idea how much I've beat myself up over that?"

"You shouldn't have." He kissed Lane's stomach. "I've never had anyone want me that badly." A wave of fear sideswiped Walker. He squeezed Lane as his heart skipped a few beats. "I don't want to lose you."

Lane stroked his face. "You won't."

Walker held his stare. He was so fucking terrified, and Lane was the only person he trusted enough to show his fear. "They say I've only got around a twenty-eight percent chance of living through this."

Lane's chest expanded, but he didn't look away. "You won't leave me."

Lane's faith was humbling. Walker crawled up his body and captured Lane's mouth. Their tongues played. Love owned Walker. Everything else fell away. His hand found its way inside Lane's underwear. He needed to make Lane feel. Walker couldn't be alone in this sea of emotions. He'd never felt so much for anyone. Lane was everything.

He needed more. Walker sat back on his heels and peeled off his shirt. The way Lane watched him through feverish eyes had Walker being rougher than he intended as he stripped away Lane's clothes. Lane didn't scoff. Still, Walker didn't want him to be nervous. "Don't be scared. I'll take care of everything."

"I'm not afraid."

Lane possessed a warrior's heart. When they

were nude, Walker straddled Lane's hips. He kept his weight balanced on his knees as he reclaimed Lane's lips. Walker was so filled with hunger and love that he didn't have room for his earlier exhaustion. His hips rolled. Their erections brushed. A stuttered gasp escaped Lane and Walker knew Lane felt the same powerful connection.

Walker palmed their cocks and thrusted. He kept his pace steady. His lips skimmed Lane's cheek. "You have no idea how much I've wanted this." Lane moaned, making Walker even hotter. "Damn. Having you in that bed next to me in Orlando was torture. All the times you've fallen asleep right where I could touch you have tested me more than anything in my life." Walker couldn't stop baring his soul. The pressure beating at his crown and knowing it was Lane beneath him was fucking with his head. "I haven't wanted anyone else since the first time we slow danced." Lane's fingers dug into his skin where he gripped Walker's shoulders, proving how the confession affected Lane. For Walker, that was his biggest secret. That first dance had been more than a year ago—long before rehab or Trace's marriage to Lane's dad. But Lane had been sober that night. His eyes had been clear and his laughter genuine. Walker hadn't looked away since. He didn't see anyone else.

He kissed the corner of Lane's mouth. Lane tried chasing him, but Walker couldn't stop baring his soul. "One day soon, I plan to fuck you. You'll beg for more."

Lane whimpered, "Please?"

The plea sounded like it came from Lane's soul. He couldn't take it. Walker had never wanted anyone's cum so badly in his life. He was half insane with desire. Walker moved fast. He shifted positions, moving down Lane's body. He swallowed Lane's cock. A cry filled the room. Lane's hips left the bed, chasing Walker's mouth. He scratched at the bed sheet while openly fucking Walker's throat. It was sexy, and Walker couldn't stop stroking himself. They were every fantasy Walker ever had. He was on the edge of explosion. The sounds Lane made had Walker hornier than he'd ever been. He wished he was inside Lane, but that would have to wait. Instead, he'd settle for the salty flavor of Lane's cum. Walker sucked harder, needing it. He needed Lane to be at the same level of insanity.

Lane's short nails scored Walker's shoulders. "Oh, fuck," Lane growled as hot cum filled Walker's mouth.

Walker squeezed his eyes closed and swallowed. His entire body strained toward release. He held his breath as he beat faster at his dick. The first wave hit, forcing the final breath of air from his lungs. Walker gasped around Lane's cock, refusing to give up his treat. He massaged every spark of pleasure out, rocking against his hand. They'd soaked Lane's sheets. A hint of pride washed over Walker as he kissed his way up Lane's body. Lane was a pool of jelly beneath him, gasping and obviously incapable of moving. He made Walker even prouder as he accepted Walker kiss with no fucks over his cum still coating Walker's tongue. They would be happy. Maybe they were in for one hell of a fight and they were starting things under the worst of circumstances, but they were stronger together. Whether Walker lived or died, he knew Lane would be there. He'd never loved anyone more.

SIX

CHEMO WAS SO MUCH WORSE than anything Lane imagined. Most days, Walker was incapable of leaving the bed. Lane had given his notice to Trace. No more waffling. As bad as he felt about leaving while Walker was also not working, Trace had been amazing. He'd quickly worked to promote Mason to manager and hire extra staff. Walker bitched about Lane giving up his life, but Lane didn't want to be anywhere else. Despite his brave face, he was scared out of his mind that Walker wouldn't make it. Thankfully, his store had an amazing staff and raked in money without him. Everything stopped for Walker. While Lane understood the doctors hoped to shrink Walker's tumor before removing it—the smaller the tumor, the less damage to Walker's brain—it was tough as hell to watch. Especially knowing, even if the surgery was successful, there'd likely be things Walker couldn't do any longer afterward. There was just no way to know what those things might be. Lane wanted every minute, every second of Walker he could get. He didn't want to miss anything.

"Baby?" Lane spoke against Walker's nape, keeping his voice low in case he'd actually dozed off.

"Hmm."

"I've been thinking."

Walker snuggled deeper into Lane's hold. "Nothing good ever starts with those words."

Lane smiled and stroked Walker's chest. He loved the sensation of Walker's heart beating against his palm. "I'm really hoping you don't feel that way in a minute. How do you feel about moving in with me? Before you answer," Lane said, rushing to get his argument in before Walker scoffed. "You living here would make it easier for me to take care of you. All your stuff would be here, and we could stop having the conversation about where we're sleeping every night. I mean, that's where we're headed anyhow, right?" Silence dragged on, making Lane doubt himself. Plus, he didn't want to stress Walker right now. "It's okay," Lane said, hearing the nervousness in his voice. "You have a lot going on, and I'm sure you still wonder sometimes if I'll end up back in rehab."

Walker rolled in Lane's hold and met his stare. He looked wide awake, which surprised Lane, considering he'd been especially sick today. He rubbed Lane's side, coming dangerously close to tickling. "I was waiting to hear your entire argument. You don't have to convince me of anything. I love you."

Happiness filled Lane. He tried tempering his reaction because he knew Walker still didn't have much energy. "I love you too."

Walker tapped his lips. "Kiss me and then go to my truck. I left a present for you in the glovebox."

Lane's brow furrowed in his confusion. "When did you have time to get me a present?" His excitement had him moving.

Laughter filled the bedroom. Walker snagged his arm before he could get away. "Whoa. Aren't you forgetting something?"

Heat exploded across his cheeks. Lane felt a bit ridiculous. No one ever bought him gifts. He straddled Walker's hips. With his weight balanced on his hands and knees, Lane lowered his head and skimmed his lips across Walker's. Walker's head left the pillow, chasing his kiss. Lane's heart turned over in his chest. Even though they were dealing with some of the worst stuff imaginable, Lane had never been deeper in love.

Walker stroked his face. "Go get your gift."

Lane scrambled from the bed. Not only was he excited about the present, he wanted to get back to Walker. He found Walker's keys and headed outside. The first wisps of fall were in the air. The leaves were turning, and the temperature was falling. He could practically feel Halloween just around the corner. After unlocking the passenger side door, Lane used the running board to climb inside. Walker's truck was too fucking high. He popped open the glovebox and found a gold bag. It was only a little bigger than his hand. There was a card sticking out the top. Lane set the bag aside and tore open the card.

On the front, there were glittery hearts and glasses of champagne. Lane flipped it open. There was only a handwritten note inside.

Lane,

I'm sure you don't remember, but we met on this day three years ago. We're not a case of love at first sight. In fact, we didn't even like each other. You thought I was cranky and bossy. I thought you were a mess. In some ways, we were both right.

Back then, I never dreamed the day would come when I'd feel like there's no me without you. If anyone would've told me I would end up completely obsessed with you, I would've laughed. My mom used to say that life loves nothing better than watching people trip over their feet and fall in love. Secretly, I always thought that was a weird saying. Until I met you.

I feel like I always take the long road or the wrong one when it comes to you. But no matter which way I turn, you're always there. If that's not proof we're meant to be, then I don't know what is. So, in celebration of the day I met the love of my life, I'd love to make it official. I don't know how much time I have, but that's true of everyone. The only thing I know is that I want to spend whatever life we have left together. I don't want to waste any minutes focused on anything but us.

I love you. It's not fair for me to ask for more, but I want everything with you. Open your gift. — Walker

Lane set the card aside and looked inside the bag. There was a tiny velvet bag inside. He dug it out. It was cinched closed with a tiny drawstring. He worked it open and dumped the contents into his hand. A diamond-encrusted band slipped out, landing in his palm. Lane wasn't sure he blinked as he stared at the object in his hand. He snatched up the card and read it again. Lane was a good ninety percent sure Walker had just proposed. With the ring clutched in his fist and the bag and card pinned against his chest, Lane jumped from the truck and headed for the door. By the time he made it inside, he was nearly jogging. He had to know. The answer was a resounding yes, but he was scared to hope and be wrong.

Lane slid into the bedroom out of breath. "Did you just—" The words died in his throat. Fear choked him into silence. Walker looked like he was sleeping, but Lane knew better. He felt the change in the air. Walker was there, but his overwhelming presence was gone. Lane rushed to the edge of the bed. "Don't you fucking dare." The words came out in a screech that sounded inhuman, even to Lane's ears. Lane was amazed how many thoughts he had in the short second it took him to get to Walker's side. He hadn't been gone that long. How was he supposed to go on? Walker couldn't go without him. Lane wasn't strong enough for this.

Touching Walker only confirmed his fears. Walker felt like there was no life in him any longer.

In his panic, Lane knocked several things from the side table. The sight of Walker's phone hitting the floor spurred Lane into action. He snatched up the device and typed in the code. There were no secrets between them. How dare Walker send him outside and die alone? He couldn't fucking do this to Lane. Lane dialed 911 and switched the phone to speaker. Everything slowed to a crawl. He checked Walker for a pulse, even though he knew he wouldn't find one. Life turned into a blur. In some detached way, Lane heard himself calling for help. He started chest compressions—like he'd been taught years ago at a long forgotten part-time job as a lifeguard. Two months in the summer. People in bathing suits. He'd been unmoved. No one affected him but Walker. Lane couldn't control his crazy random thoughts. It was like his brain was trying to find a way to cope with reality. The reality was Walker was gone, and Lane had nothing left to keep him here. Getting clean had been useless. All the nights he'd suffered just to live another day were meaningless. He'd lost the only person who mattered. Lane wouldn't survive it. He didn't intend to try.

SEVEN

PEOPLE KEPT TALKING TO LANE. He didn't hear a word. Someone hugged him. Lane couldn't recall two seconds later who it had been. All he could think about was all the things Walker and he had missed. Walker had been so sick, they hadn't really made love. Not the way they wanted. Walker had been determined to ease Lane into the penetrative sex that they hadn't tried. They'd done other things. Less taxing forms of lovemaking, but now Lane hated they'd never done more. They'd acted like they had all the time in the world, even as they'd known that wasn't the case. Now he recognized all that he'd missed.

He'd managed to restore a heartbeat long enough for paramedics to arrive. From there, they'd placed

Walker on life support. His doctor had decided they couldn't wait any longer to remove the tumor. Size was no longer as important as the parts of the brain the tumor pressed on. Walker would die without the surgery. With it, he didn't stand much of a chance either, but slim odds were better than none. Hours upon hours of held breath and waiting had produced nothing but more waiting. Until the only news he'd gotten was Walker hadn't woken after the surgery. If he ever woke up, they couldn't say if there'd be anything left of the Walker that Lane knew.

Still, Lane sat and waited. Sometimes, he dozed only long enough for nightmares to grip him. Then he was back to waiting. Life screeched to a halt. Occasionally, he stared at the wall or whatever was on the TV left there by whoever visited last. Most of the time, Lane watched Walker's every breath and prayed to see his eyes again. He could never, ever go through another round of trying to restart Walker's heart.

Fifteen of the longest days of Lane's life passed before those sexy, sweet brown eyes locked on Lane again. The elation that brought Lane to his feet lasted all of five seconds.

"Why are you here?"

Lane blinked. Although hard to understand due

to the scratchiness of Walker's voice, Lane was positive he heard right. "Um. Waiting for you to wake up. How are you feeling, baby?"

A line appeared between Walker's eyes. "My head hurts. I'm not your baby. What happened to me?"

Lane sat. Rather, his knees gave out. "What do you remember?" Lane thought he would puke. Walker looked at him like he was a stranger.

Walker blinked several times. "Trace and I worked later than usual, and then nothing."

The nurse came in before Lane could ask more questions. His mind raced. Walker and Trace hadn't worked late together in well over a year. If that was the last thing Walker remembered, then he didn't remember being with Lane. The past year they'd been together was gone. Walker had lived. Lane hadn't lost him. Yet, somehow, Lane had still lost him. He didn't understand how one person could be so relieved and crushed at the same time.

EVERYONE KEPT STARING AT HIM. WALKER STILL hadn't come to grips with reality. Trace had tried filling in the blanks of Walker's missing memories, but nothing felt real. Other than the pain, he still believed he'd stayed up late with Trace, gone to bed, and woken up in the hospital the next morning. But other things were missing too beyond the past year or so. Like he couldn't remember his mom. He was certain he had one. Everyone did. His dad was still in there, for the most part, but his mom was gone. Only Trace kept him sane by filling the gaps. His parents had passed years ago. His middle name was Paul. Walker hadn't worked in months, Lane was the greatest love of his life, and Walker didn't recall a damn thing about any of that. The more he stewed over not knowing, the more his rage grew. It was like a sick joke.

"Could you leave?"

Lane's gaze met Walker's at the demand. He hadn't stopped looking like Walker beat the fuck out of him since Walker woke. Walker couldn't take it any longer. It was too much. He was angry. It felt like everyone played a horrible prank, except there wasn't a goddamn thing funny about any of it.

Trace was the one who spoke first. "Walker, Lane's been here—"

"It's fine," Lane said, coming to his feet. "I'm making things worse."

"Lane..." Trace sounded like he was witnessing the greatest of tragedies.

Lane waved off Trace's concerns. He shook his head, as if begging Trace to let it go. Lane didn't meet anyone's stare. His gaze swept the room, as if he fought to decide where to look while barely holding himself together. He cleared his throat. "If you need anything, my number is programmed in your phone."

Walker didn't respond. The guilt was real, but so too was the fury. Walker wanted his life back. The real one. Not the fake bullshit everyone tried feeding him. Walker stayed focused on Trace while Trace watched Lane leave.

As soon as they were alone, Trace focused on him. The disappointment in Trace's eyes had Walker ready to tear his hair out, except that was gone too. Trace didn't say the words, because he was too good for that, but Walker saw it all in the man's eyes. Walker was a piece of shit who'd kicked out a man who'd done nothing but love Walker for over a year, caring for him through a deadly illness. Hell, Lane had even brought him back to life when his fucked-up brain had forgotten how to breathe under the pressure of a brain tumor. The thing was, Walker was all fucked up. His chest hurt and his emotions were all over the place. He felt things, but they didn't make sense because he couldn't remember them. Walker needed space. Trace was too nice.

He stood. "I'm sure you'd like a minute to yourself. Everyone's been staring at since you woke up. I'll come back later tonight. If you need anything before then, you know how to reach me."

Walker nodded while choking on his tongue. He wanted to scream and never stop. When he was alone, Walker squeezed his eyes closed. At one time, he'd known about a tumor slowly killing him. He'd had time to deal and accept. But he'd forgotten all that and now what he'd dealt with in a year, he had to grasp all over again. He was fucking trying. His chest felt funny. Not like heart attack weird, but like his heart was breaking, and he didn't know why. Common sense said it was because he'd almost died, but that excuse wasn't adding up in his head. He stared into space, listening to the hands on the clock tick. Time passed with no input from Walker until madness threatened to overcome him.

"Hey, man. I heard you were awake and ready for visitors. I had to come see for myself." Mason sailed into the room like he owned the place, the way Mason did everything.

It was a breath of fresh air to have someone loud and happy who wasn't looking at him like he'd keel over at any moment. "Hey. It's good to see you. I'm surprised you don't have Dillion with you."

Mason winced as he snagged the chair by the bed. "They warned me you'd forgotten a lot. Dillion went to check on Lane." Walker's hand automatically went to his chest. He rubbed, trying to knead away the sudden aching. Mason kept talking like nothing happened. "But I'll be sure to let Dillion know you've forgotten you hate him so he can come visit too."

Walker already wanted Mason to leave. It was like there was no one who didn't remind him of the missing pieces. "Maybe it's best I don't know. Tell me what I've missed with you instead."

Mason shrugged. His eyes danced with laughter the way they always did. People flocked to Mason, hoping to soak up whatever he possessed that obviously made him not need anyone else to be content. "I'm the manager at Incubus now. That's pretty sweet. Otherwise," Mason shrugged again, "you know me. So, when are you getting sprung?"

"No clue. I imagine it'll be a long while, though. There are still tests, and god knows what, depending on what they learn."

Mason nodded along, looking more serious than Walker could recall. "At least you have Lane. He'll make sure you're taken care of, no matter how long it takes."

"No." Walker didn't bother softening his tone.

Mason's brows drew together, showing his obvious confusion. "Okay. That's... Okay." A sad smile touched Mason's lips. He shook his head. "Cancer sucks, man. I worried about you, thinking you might not make it, but never in a million years did I expect this. No way did I think it would tear you from Lane in this way. After the months of being glued to each other through his doctor's appointments, and both of you fighting through each other's illnesses, never did I think you'd choose to leave him to fight alone. That's the saddest fucking thing I've ever heard."

"What illness?"

Mason shook his head again. "I'm done. I shouldn't have said anything at all. Not my business. You've got way too much going on right now. Tell me how I can help. Do you need me to run errands? Grab some stuff from your apartment? Sneak you some good food in? Hit me with your requests."

Walker floundered. He didn't know how to ask for anything when he wasn't sure about anything. For all he knew, he lived with Lane. Or maybe he had a whole new wardrobe or was on a special diet.

He didn't know himself at all. "Could you check on Lane for me?" Walker had no idea where the request came from, but he didn't take it back. "Please?"

Mason's smile turned genuine. He stood. "That I can do."

"Don't tell him I sent you." Walker wasn't ready for that. He wasn't even sure why he cared. Maybe it was guilt. All Walker knew was nothing felt right. Knowing Mason would look in on Lane helped, so he didn't question himself. He would deal with everything later. Until then, he'd just try to get better.

Mason opened the door to leave and nearly mowed down Dillion. His gaze slid past Mason, dismissing him before landing on Walker. He didn't wait to be invited in. Dillion pushed his way past Mason using an overnight bag as his weapon to move the man who outweighed him by at least fifty pounds.

He set the bag in the chair by the bed. "Your doctor told Lane you need some comfortable clothes, so you're not forced to sit around in a gown all the time, since you'll be here a while."

"Why would my doctor tell Lane anything?" Walker didn't mean to sound like a dick, but there it was.

Light green eyes shifted his way. Walker swore he felt the distaste. "I know you recently had a brain tumor cut out, but don't be dumb *and* mean, it's not a good look, especially since Lane is the one paying for your care." He pulled a few books and ink pens from the bag and set them on the tray in front of Walker as if he hadn't knocked the air from Walker's lungs. "Your doctor also said, since you're left-handed, you really need to work on getting the strength back on that side. He said puzzle books—like word searches and crosswords—would be the perfect way to help you work on your small motor skills while exercising your brain. So do these puzzles." Dillion straightened, eyed the things he'd brought, and then nodded sharply as if satisfied he'd delivered as instructed. "Anything else? No? Good. Get well soon." Dillion said the words fast, obviously uncaring if Walker actually needed anything else.

"How did Lane get into my apartment?" Walker asked before Dillion could make a clean getaway. If they lived together, Walker needed to know that.

With one foot out the door, Dillion turned and met his stare. "He didn't. Everything I brought is what you already had at his place. There's no need for you to worry that he's stealing everything not nailed down at yours. Despite your shoddy treatment and obvious hatred, he still loves you." His gaze slid Mason's way. After eyeing the man from head to foot, he focused on Walker once more. "Treating people like shit who've done the most for you seems to be most men's MO, so whatever. Like I said, get well soon." He disappeared without another backward glance. Funny how his "get well soon" sounded more like "fuck you."

For a moment, Walker blinked at the spot where Dillion had been before his gaze slid Mason's way. "What in the hell was that all about?"

Mason shifted from one foot to the other, looking uncomfortable as hell. "Um, well. I guess you forgot you two had a falling out."

"Seriously?" Walker couldn't believe it. He'd always liked Dillion.

Mason nodded. He looked more defeated by the second. "You had him arrested after he got into a fight at Incubus and keyed my truck. Of course, his lawyers got the whole thing tossed out, and Trace refused to let you ban him from the club. The whole thing left you with the opinion he's an entitled twat."

Walker was fairly certain his jaw dropped. "Are you fucking kidding me?"

Mason's gaze slid away. "To be fair, it was my fault. You were sticking up for me." Mason finally focused on Walker once more. He looked resigned. "You shouldn't have, though."

Walker scrubbed his face. He'd lost so much. Too much to keep up with. "Let me guess—you've been sleeping with Dillion but can't keep your dick in your jeans."

The way Mason shifted from foot to foot and wouldn't meet his stare said everything Walker needed to know. Goddamn, he was tired. He had too much of his own shit going on for this. Maybe he'd wake up tomorrow and find out all this really had been a horrible dream. Walker doubted it, but at this point, hoping for a nightmare was the only lifeline he had left.

EIGHT

LANE: *You had some mail come to my place. I gave it to Trace.*

LANE: *A PHYSICAL THERAPIST CALLED ME, SAYING you need to set up three appointments a week for six weeks after you're released. I said I'd pass along the message.*

WALKER: *TRACE SAYS YOU KNOW WHERE MY keys are.*

    Lane: *Are you going home?*

Lane: **sigh** *They're in that blue bag I packed for you.*

LANE: *I PICKED UP ALL YOUR PRESCRIPTIONS AND gave them to Trace. He'll pass them along.*

WALKER STARED AT HIS PHONE. AS HE'D DONE dozens of times since waking up with half a life, he scrolled back through his messages with Lane. It was so fucking odd. He stared at his life, but it wasn't him. The messages between Lane and him were adorable. He behaved in a way with Lane he'd never acted with anyone else. Not that he recalled anyhow. There were pictures too. A blushing Lane getting caught off guard. Kisses. An intimate video. They were in love—just as everyone said. Walker didn't know how to reconcile what his eyes showed him and what he knew. At least, what he knew now.

The thing was, sometimes, Walker woke, and right before he fully grasped consciousness, he would reach for Lane. The disappointment was real each time he found his bed empty. Occasionally, in the middle of the night, confusion would pull him from his dreams. For a split second, he couldn't figure out why the weight of Lane's head on his chest was missing. Before he could cling to what his brain wanted him to remember, the moment was gone. Yet he couldn't stop staring at Lane's pictures. Walker couldn't explain the desperation that grew each day in his chest.

"You should go see him."

Walker quickly closed the photo app on his phone as Trace filled the loveseat next to him. He'd taken a cab to Incubus to hang out with Trace before the club opened, because he couldn't stand his four walls pressing in on him anymore.

"I don't want to give him false hope," Walker admitted as he accepted the bottle of water Trace held out.

Trace shrugged. "Who knows? You fell for him once. It could happen again. I don't think it was a fluke."

Walker nodded and turned the bottle up, killing half of it before responding. "I shouldn't put you in this position. Lane is your stepson now, which still blows me away, by the way."

A sexy-sounding chuckle rumbled from Trace.

"For a while there, I thought you might be my stepson-in-law. Now that's mind boggling."

Walker laughed at the idea even as a pang of loss sideswiped him.

"I love you," Trace added, making the pains worse. "I'm glad you're still with us. Everything else will find a way."

Walker flashed a smile he didn't feel. Everything felt... wrong. There was something missing, and he was scared he knew exactly what it was, but if it wasn't, then he was about to ruin Lane's life all over again. From what Walker understood, from everyone else and reading their texts, Lane might not survive another blow. But the "I love you" lingering on his lips had nowhere to go. The empty pit in his stomach couldn't be filled. Walker needed to see Lane. He couldn't ignore his gut any longer. Walker just prayed he wasn't making a mistake. Otherwise, he might kill the person he loved the most while incapable of remembering why.

THE SOLITUDE AND SILENCE WERE YAWNING, making Lane's apartment feel like a tomb. His legs ached from pacing the floor. Walker had gone home from the hospital. Trace kept Lane posted. They both knew it was a pointless chore at this point. Walker didn't call or text. He hadn't since waking up. Not really. Looking for his keys didn't count. Trace had reluctantly admitted Walker never asked about him. It was an odd feeling, knowing he existed, yet he didn't—not to Walker.

His last Fibro flare-up had been the worst one yet. Lane couldn't tell if he was getting worse or if he'd given up. In truth, either way, he was finished fighting. Lane checked his phone. Even though he knew there wouldn't be any new texts from Walker, he liked looking through their old messages. Maybe he would delete them. There were so many I love yous. They were lies now.

No one understood. The months Walker had spent helping Lane find a diagnosis, he'd more than saved Lane. He'd believed Lane. While everyone else thought he was an addict looking for a new way to get more drugs, Walker had listened to Lane and believed. Now he was gone. The only reason Lane had to stay sober and strong was gone. There was nothing left for him anymore.

Lane wasn't angry. It was no one's fault. He didn't know if he felt worse or better because there was no one to blame. Not that it mattered. Lane was tired. He couldn't fake one more smile. Each time someone knocked on his door, forcing him to play nice, Lane thought he'd scream. His throat hurt too badly. It turned out swallowing the tears was hell on the vocal chords. He didn't want to talk to anyone. Lane didn't want to keep lying about being okay. He'd paced the floor so much, he'd worn down the varnish, but he couldn't go to bed. Lane wanted to be left alone, but his bed was too lonely.

As if the universe heard his pain and decided to hand him more, someone knocked on the door. Lane kept pacing. There was no law that said he had to answer. The knock came again and again until Lane gave up and threw open the door. The rage building in his chest bled away instantly. Walker stood on the other side.

He flashed Lane a small smile. Lane couldn't tear his eyes away. The love was still there, choking him. There was no such thing as too much time or distance. Lane would always love him.

"I found my way here. Well, I remembered how to give a cabbie directions." Walker looked so fucking uncomfortable and Lane could barely breathe. He wanted to find hope in Walker's claim. Hopelessness was too ingrained.

Lane cleared his throat and took a step back.

"Come in. Sorry about the mess." Lane looked at everything but Walker. It hurt too much. His arms ached without Walker to hold. No way could he look directly at what he could never have.

Walker stepped inside but didn't move any farther into the room. He stood just inside the doorway, as if he might make a run for it at any moment. "You know, I didn't forget you on purpose."

At the hurt in Walker's voice, Lane finally made his eyes focus on the man. "I know. It's okay." It wasn't, but what else could he say? Lane took a breath. "You're alive. That's all that matters." His mouth kept saying words and Lane couldn't connect with any of them. This was why he needed to get as far away as he could from this place, the people, and the memories.

Walker looked around. "What's up with all the boxes?"

"I'm moving." Lane didn't know what to do with his hands, so he clasped them behind his back. "My store sold faster than I expected, but I'll be out in time for the new owners. A local charity will come for my things tomorrow. Don't worry. I gave Trace the money to pay off the rest of your hospital bill."

"I don't care about that." Of course he didn't, because it was all Lane had to offer, and Walker didn't want Lane. "Where are you going?" Walker sounded like he cared. Lane wished he wouldn't.

"Away."

Walker's brow furrowed. "Do you not want to tell me, or do you not know?"

Neither. Lane's lips wouldn't form the truth. He wasn't sure they knew how any longer. "I guess I'll probably travel for a while. You look well." He just wanted to talk about anything else.

Walker nodded. "I'm good. I mean, I still have a ways to go. Physical therapy and relearning things—like how to drive. Trace says you meant everything to me. Actually, everyone keeps telling me that."

It was like being sideswiped by a bus. Lane looked away. He couldn't do this. His gaze landed on the small box of items that belonged to Walker. He crossed the room and grabbed it. "This is yours. I'd planned to give it to Trace to pass along, but since you're here." He held the box out to Walker without looking at him. Walker's sweet brown eyes were killing Lane. How much else did he have to endure?

"Thanks." Walker accepted the box.

Lane noticed he still wasn't using his left hand much. He forced his gaze away again. Walker's health was no longer his business.

Walker eyed the contents of the small box. He

set it at his feet and pulled out the small velvet bag. Lane turned away. He worried he'd start screaming and then never stop. "There was a card with this."

Lane spun so fast, he made himself dizzy.

Walker stared down at the ring. "Right?"

It was like a bucket of cold water was tossed in his face at the uncertainty in Walker's voice. Walker didn't remember and that split second of hope was too much. He grabbed the card from where it stayed on the coffee table. The edges were frayed from all the times Lane held it and cried. He handed it to Walker. "Here, I guess it belongs to you too."

Lane's knees almost buckled as Walker took the card from his fingers. The last piece of Walker was gone from him now. It was for the best. Still, his heart screamed a thousand denials.

Walker opened the card. His gaze moved over the words. "I don't remember writing this, even though it's obvious I did." Each time Lane thought there was nothing left of him to break, Walker found new pieces to shatter.

"It's okay." Lane didn't know why he kept saying that. It wasn't okay. It would never, ever be okay.

Walker's gaze lifted. His light brown stare still made Lane weak, even as it kept him held in place. "The thing is," Walker said, setting the card back on the table. "Even though I don't remember, I still feel you. I still know you're missing from me." The loud thump of Lane's heartbeat pounded in his ears as he watched Walker move closer. "Every single night, I wake up and there's a wisp of you before it slips away, and I know that I've lost something important. My body burns and I know it's for you, even though I don't recall why."

Lane swallowed—hard. "Okay." Fuck. He didn't know what else to say.

Walker stopped inches from Lane, hovering over him and forcing Lane to tilt his chin up to meet Walker's stare. "Do you think it would be okay if I kissed you? I don't want to hurt you any more than I already have, but I need to know."

Without thought, Lane's hands slid across Walker's hips, the way they always did right before Walker kissed him. Walker shuffled closer. Lane held still, waiting. His eyes slipped closed as Walker dipped his chin. Their lips met, brushed, and moved away. Then Lane's head fell back as Walker took control. Lane surrendered under the assault of his kiss. Walker sucked Lane's tongue and kissed him deep. His hands moved from Lane's waist to his ass. He hauled Lane closer until the lower half of their bodies collided. Lane moved restlessly against

Walker, needing him. His body screamed for more while his brain demanded Lane stop before he lost a part of himself he couldn't survive without. Then Lane remembered that part of him was already gone. He'd already given up. Lane already had no intention of continuing on. This kiss was just one more thing that soon wouldn't matter. Even as Lane's jeans loosened beneath Walker's touch, Lane didn't deny him. It was Walker. Lane's body belonged to him.

"Where's the bedroom?" Walker growled the words against Lane's lips. He sounded desperate. Lane couldn't deny him. With his gaze locked on his feet, Lane took Walker's hand and headed for the bedroom. One night together wouldn't change anything.

As they stepped across the threshold into Lane's bedroom, Walker's arms encircled Lane. He drew Lane back against his chest. "I still feel you," he whispered against Lane's throat as he pushed Lane's pants and underwear down his hips. "I have dreams of you holding me. You're still inside me somewhere. Help me find you."

Lane gasped for air. He needed this. Maybe Walker would leave afterward, and it would be the final blow, but Lane was already dead inside. He needed to have Walker's hands on his body. Walker didn't let him down. He massaged every place he could reach while stripping Lane. In what felt like a matter of seconds, Lane found himself nude and stretched out on the bed face down. His brain refused to work properly with all his blood elsewhere. Walker kissed and bit a path down Lane's body until his teeth sank into Lane's ass. Lane squeezed his eyes closed. He savored every sensation. Lubed fingers probed at his asshole. By memory or not, it seemed Walker had found the drawer next to the bed.

There was still a piece of Lane that clung to his heartache, even as Walker set Lane's body on fire. If Walker remembered anything about them, Lane didn't think Walker would be so set on this. They'd made love, but not like this. It was the first time Lane was glad Walker didn't know about them. Lane had regretted not having this above all else. No matter what happened afterward, Lane would hold tonight to his chest.

"You're beautiful," Walker whispered against the small of Lane's back. Lane heard and felt every word.

The fingers pumping inside his ass, massaging the perfect spot, had Lane moving restlessly against the bed. It was Walker touching him and his body knew its owner had come home. Walker urged Lane's hips up. He slid a thick pillow beneath him, positioning Lane how he liked. Lane let everything happen to him. He was helpless against Walker. If there was even the slightest chance Walker still loved him, even just a little, Lane needed it. If not, Lane wanted the chance to lie to himself for a moment. Any relief from the loss was something.

Walker went back to playing. Lane focused on every sensation. His hips rolled without thought, seeking more and moving closer to the edge. Something much larger pressed against his asshole, seeking entry. Lane tried to relax. Walker thrust. Lane bit the sheet. The pain was worse than he expected. Walker held still, whispering praise that Lane barely heard. He tried unclenching his muscles. Walker rocked against him. Lane forced himself to breathe. Then Walker changed angles. He pounded the perfect spot. Lane's body turned to jelly as he focused on the building pleasure. His cock felt neglected, but the building tension from behind held him in place. He let Walker's thrusts rock him into the pillow, slightly stimulating his erection while giving him all the internal pleasure. His mind was blissfully blank as the things happening to his body held his entire focus. They were perfect while locked together. Lane had always known they would be.

"Fuck, Lane. You're too perfect. I need you to come. You're killing me. It's like this hole is only for me."

The backs of Lane's eyes burned. His body didn't care Lane's heart was broken. Pressure pounded at his crown, needing release. He squeezed his eyes shut and focused on the light brush of the pillow on his dick and the pressure of Walker's cock punching his internal button. He strained toward the promise of ecstasy. His muscles clenched. A strangled cry sounded above him. Lane gasped for air. Lights popped behind his closed eyelids. The first wave hit, stealing a moan from deep within Lane's soul. It sounded a lot like Walker's name. Muttered words tore from Lane as he writhed beneath Walker's dick, trying to suck the man deeper and hold on to him forever. The guttural cursing above him sounded like the most beautiful music to Lane. He memorized every note.

Walker's weight collapsed onto Lane. Lane absorbed it as his due. It didn't matter he couldn't breathe. He hadn't breathed properly in months. Nothing mattered except the soft kisses brushing the shell of his ear. The love he'd been trying to rip away from himself was clawing Lane's guts, tearing away at his insides, and demanding recognition. Lane ignored the pounding at his skull—the traitorous thoughts that tried breaking free, reminding him Walker was no longer his.

Walker's weight disappeared. Cold air washed over his skin. Lane kept his face hidden. The bed shifted as Walker rolled from the bed. Tears threatened to spill over Lane's lashes. Soon. It would be over soon.

The bed shifted again. "Come here." Walker rolled Lane into his arms. Lane clenched his back teeth, willing himself not to cry as he focused on Walker's face. Before Lane had time to fall apart, Walker's mouth covered his. He kissed Lane so sweetly, Lane couldn't think of anything else. Walker urged his knees apart. He gently cleaned away their mess while keeping Lane distracted by their kiss. "I don't want you to cry," Walker whispered between kisses. He tossed the washcloth aside and wiped the tears away Lane hadn't known were falling. "I'm not going anywhere. Whether the memories come back or not, I'm not the kind of guy who leaves."

Lane nodded. Walker wasn't that guy. He wouldn't leave. Not tonight anyhow. Tomorrow, things might change, but Lane would take tonight.

He held tight and soaked in every caress. For one more night, Lane would pretend he might survive. His heart knew the truth, though. This had been goodbye. Walker loving him had always been a fluke. It wouldn't happen twice, and the truth of the matter was this: Lane couldn't live without Walker. He wouldn't try.

THE BED SHIFTED SLIGHTLY, PULLING WALKER from sleep. "Baby?" Walker searched for Lane in the dark.

He saw Lane's outline freeze in front of the soft light spilling from the nightlight in the bathroom. "Yeah?"

"It's too late to be up writing." Even Walker heard the slur to his voice. In truth, he was more asleep than awake.

"I'm just going to the bathroom."

Walker rolled onto his back. "Oh, okay. Hurry back. I've missed holding you at night."

Lane sniffed. "Okay." His answer sounded garbled. Walker shook off sleep and sat up. He turned on the bedside lamp. Lane stood nude at the foot of the bed. His eyes were bloodshot, and tears streamed down his face, but he didn't look away from Walker or try to hide.

"What wrong, baby?"

"You remembered that I get up to write at night."

Walker was still waking up, making him slow on the uptake. He realized Lane was right. He couldn't know what he didn't know, but memories of them crowded his head. The overwhelming sense of loss he'd been dealing with since waking up in the hospital made sense now. This was what he had been missing.

Walker's throat swelled. When he spoke, his voice cracked. "I never would've forgotten you on purpose."

Lane cried harder. He covered his mouth but made no move to wipe the tears away. "I lost you. You left me."

There was too much info at once. Walker tried processing. It was like waking up in the middle of the night with Lane had reconnected the wires in his brain. "You sold your store. Where were you going without me? You planned to leave."

Lane shook his head. He gasped for air. "I wasn't strong without you."

"Where were you going?"

"Nowhere. I wasn't strong."

It dawned on Walker what Lane meant. He was selling off his stuff, using the money to pay for Walker's care, and then he planned to... die? He'd planned to check out. Walker couldn't breathe. What would've happened if he hadn't shown up tonight? What if he hadn't remembered? Walker stared at Lane in shocked silence. "You can't do that to me. How could you even consider doing that to me?"

Lane's hands rose before falling to his sides in a helpless motion. "You didn't know me. You can't lose what you don't miss."

Helplessness overwhelmed Walker. Walker opened his arms. He had nothing else to offer but his love, but he did love Lane.

Lane crawled onto the bed and into Walker's hold.

"I'm so sorry I failed you. I swore I wouldn't let you suffer, and that's exactly what happened." When Walker's arms closed around Lane, he could feel Lane shaking. He shook so hard, it rattled Walker's teeth. Walker snagged the covers and tucked them around Lane while holding on tight. He'd been so angry since waking up. Before now, he hadn't understood why. At first, he'd thought he was mad at Lane—like Lane pulled some cruel prank by pretending they were together. Now he realized he was pissed off for Lane. Lane had dealt with so much. It was cruel for life to hand him Walker too. A man who could take care of Lane should've been the one to win him. Not Walker. Yet, here they were, and Walker would kill anyone who tried to come between them. They were a team. Walker remembered. He wouldn't forget again.

He kissed Lane's ear, cheek, and the corner of his mouth. Walker couldn't stop kissing every place he could reach. Slowly, the shaking faded. Walker kept holding him and rocking him, trying to take away the hurt. He would do this as long as it took.

Walker had never felt worse. Lane was the greatest love of his life and everything had been stripped from them. "I only wanted to love you." Walker's voice cracked on the confession. "I never meant to break you." Hot tears pressed at the backs of Walker's eyes. He fully understood everyone's horror over Walker's inability to remember Lane. They were a set. Soul mates not meant to be apart. Life had been so cruel to Lane, stealing his mother, forcing an incurable and painful disorder upon him, before saddling him with Walker.

As the past year and a half filled him, so too did the horror. He stared down at Lane. His red eyes and nose only made him more beautiful. Walker blinked, trying to come to grips with reality. "Dear God." The horrified whisper rasped from his throat, coming from his soul. "Why in the hell did you let me make love to you like that? Did I hurt you? Fuck, Lane. You should've said something."

A stuttered breath escaped Lane, sounding like a small child. It tore at Walker's heart. "Because I lost you."

Walker felt like his chest caved. He'd been purposely waiting to make love to Lane until he had time to adjust. Walker had wanted everything to be perfect. In fact, he'd kind of wanted to wait until they were married, which was a ridiculous little dream of his. But he'd wanted what he wanted, and now he'd probably ensured Lane never wanted to try again. He couldn't breathe. Walker sucked air. He didn't realize he was half-ass hyperventilating until Lane jumped to his knees and straddled Walker's lap.

Lane cupped his face. "Take a breath, sexy. I'm okay. You didn't hurt me. I wanted what I thought I'd never have since you didn't want me anymore. You didn't do anything wrong."

The sight of Lane's gorgeous eyes helped center Walker. He gasped for air. "Sorry. FYI, I have panic attacks now. Sorry you ended up with someone who's such a mess."

A huffed laugh escaped Lane. He dropped his forehead to Walker's shoulder and clung to his chest. Walker wrapped his arms around Lane and held on. "I love you."

Walker held even tighter. "I love you too."

Lane kissed his shoulder. "What do we do now?"

"Keep fighting, I guess." Walker honestly didn't know. It felt like he'd woken from a bad dream and now he just wanted to go back to real life. Life with Lane.

"We're unemployed."

"And you're homeless," Walker pointed out.

He felt Lane nod. "I think we should stick together. You know, for survival's sake."

A smile tugged at Walker's lips. They moved at the same time, touching temples. "You never answered my card."

"I didn't get a chance to ask if it was a proposal."

Walker chuckled. He loved this man so much. "You know it was."

"You know the answer was always yes." He could hear the smile in Lane's voice.

Walker nodded. He had always known. They

were meant to be. "I think we should do it now, before life throws anything else our way."

Lane nodded. He brushed his lips across Walker's, and then he did it a second time. The third time, he didn't move away. Walker's hands slid across Lane's back. The fact that they were nude slowly penetrated Walker's over-stressed brain. Lane moved restlessly against him.

"Walker." The desperate plea in Lane's voice nearly broke Walker. The madness wasn't about sex. Walker understood. It was a three-month separation while Walker fought his way back. It was the long months of push and pull before settling into a life together, only to lose everything they'd built. It was vulnerability, being ripped open—left raw and exposed. Left to die. Lane needed Walker to fix that. Fix them.

"I'll make it better. You'll see." He rolled and tucked Lane beneath him. "You'll see," he swore again before reclaiming Lane's lips. He was still lost in a huge ocean of missing pieces, but one massive chunk fell into place. Walker loved Lane. He loved Lane more than his own life. Walker needed Lane to feel it—to know his existence mattered to Walker and Walker wouldn't make it without him. He needed Lane to be whole. "Don't you ever think about leaving me again," Walker growled, on the verge of losing his shit. He had no world without Lane. Walker didn't know if Lane could breathe beneath his weight, but he couldn't give Lane space.

Lane's hips lifted. His ankles locked around the small of Walker's back. "Need you," Lane begged, writhing beneath him. "Everything is empty."

Walker understood. They weren't whole apart. His fingers dug into Lane's ass as he ground down, sending waves of pleasure down his body. "Give me everything," Walker begged, feeling half insane. His body burned. His heart ached yet it was full. It was like they'd been forcibly kept apart for years and Walker had gotten back his love. His left side was still weak, and it made itself known. Still, Walker didn't stop rocking against the sexy man beneath him. The friction between them wasn't nearly enough, but Walker needed this connection. He needed to make love to his man.

Sharp gasps escaped Lane. Walker could feel his strain. Feel him winding tighter. A stuttered breath brushed Walker's ear and Lane shook. Hot cum filled the space between them. Tiny mewling noises sounded hot as hell falling from Lane's lips. Walker wanted the moment to last forever. His body didn't care what his mind wanted. It burned. The pressure building in his shaft exploded into pops of lightning. He babbled and kissed every place he could reach, riding out the storm. Lane held tight. They were locked together by sweat and cum. By love and desperation. They were fucking beautiful together.

NINE

THE HOUSEWARMING PARTY wasn't their idea. In fact, Walker and Lane were still in a stage where they wanted to be left alone to savor their new wedding vows. Lane's dad had insisted they needed new stuff, since Lane had given all his things to charity. Walker wasn't the type to argue with his new father-in-law. Still, Walker couldn't tear his gaze away from Lane as he moved from person to person, ensuring they didn't need anything. Years of working behind a bar had transformed Lane into the perfect host. Of course, to Walker, Lane was perfect in every way. Things would be even better if everyone would leave so he could have Lane all to himself.

"Ha."

Walker glanced over at Mason's loud laugh.

Mason pointed at the fresh tattoo across Walker's bicep. "Property of Lane. That's cute."

A smile snapped to Walker's lips. "I wanted to do something that said 'if lost please return to my owner,' with Lane's name and our address, but you never know when you'll move or whatever."

"Lane could just buy you a collar."

Walker sipped his water. "Who says I don't already own one." It was worth it to see Mason's expression. His eyebrows shot up and his gaze slid away—like he'd gotten way more than he'd bargained for by pursuing this conversation. Walker chuckled.

Lane appeared beside him. "What'd I miss?"

Walker didn't answer until after he'd stolen a quick taste of the spot beneath Lane's ear. He loved that spot. "Mhmm. We were talking about my tattoo."

"Ooh, the sexy tattoo I didn't want you to get, but you insisted."

A laugh stuck in Walker's throat at the humor in Lane's voice. Lane hadn't wanted Walker to go through the pain of a tattoo, because he was too sweet, but in the end, Lane had caved. Then, once it healed, Lane had traced every letter with his tongue before licking the rest of Walker's body. Walker took a breath at the memory. The last thing he wanted was to spend the day hiding an erection.

"This is a nice place," Mason said, pulling Walker's reluctant attention back his way. "I'm thinking about buying too."

"Really?" It was awful, but Walker wasn't truly listening to Mason. He only kept Mason talking so it looked like he noticed something other than the way Lane's hair was starting to curl at the ends. He needed a haircut. Walker wanted to fuck him. Hard. Surely there was at least one room they hadn't christened yet. They should check.

"Yeah. I met this guy at work, and he's been looking for a place. Since I'm sick of renting, I think I might go ahead and buy. He said he'd split the payment."

"Sounds smart." Walker was just throwing words out there. He wanted Lane alone. The way Lane's eyes flashed with mischief said his sexy husband knew it too. Walker had never been more addicted in his life. He couldn't be more led around by his cock if Lane tied a leash around it. Walker knew the truth, though. It was his heart Lane had wrapped around his finger. Since Lane had already sold his business, they'd decided to buy a house near Trace. Walker still had healing to do. Lane had made enough on the sale of his store he could stay home and play nurse for Walker. Speaking of which, Walker thought he might be in need of Lane's care.

"I'm also thinking I should buy a dragon."

Walker's head whipped around at Mason's claim. "What?"

Mason's eyes swam with laughter. "I've been listing mythological creatures for five minutes. Truth be told, I'm a little jealous. No one has ever made me deaf before."

Heat bloomed in Walker's face. He cast a look around the room. His gaze landed on Dillion. The tiny guy looked like he tried to make himself smaller as he slipped behind Trace to hide in the corner. "I don't know. I can think of at least one person who makes you dumb."

Mason's retort lost out to Lane taking Walker's hand and leading him away. Walker followed like the lovesick fool he was without a backward glance.

"I have a surprise for you," Lane said over his shoulder.

Walker couldn't look away. Sometimes, it was like Lane cast a spell on him, keeping him enchanted and willing to do anything. "Okay."

Lane led Walker inside one of the spare bedrooms. They hadn't lived there long enough to do much decorating, but the room was furnished. A box sat on the bed. Lane motioned toward it. "For you."

For a moment, Walker stared at Lane, making no move toward the gift. He was tiny and beautiful. Walker wanted to hold him and protect him. Fibro made it hard for Lane to gain any weight. He looked fragile and angelic. Lane looked like he belonged to Walker.

Lane's mouth lifted in the corners in a shy smile. "Stop staring and open your gift." His eyes skirted away, making Walker's hunger grow. He loved that he could make Lane blush with only a look.

Walker took mercy on him and turned his attentions to the box. He lifted the lid. There were picture albums and framed photos stacked inside. Walker inspected the first set of images. It was a woman around his age. She had soft brown eyes and curly brown hair. Walker couldn't look away for reasons he couldn't explain.

"It's your mom," Lane said at his side. "I tracked down your aunt in Burbank. She apologized for not visiting, but she's on a fixed budget. I convinced her to send you some pictures of your family. This way, even if you never get back those memories, you'll still know her."

Emotions clogged Walker's throat. There was no

one else like Lane. Not for Walker anyhow. He worked and fought harder for Walker than anyone else ever had. Walker would always do the same.

With his tongue still preventing him from speaking, Walker shifted through the box's contents. There was an album filled with pictures from a trip to Disney World with Lane. They looked happy and in love, even though Lane insisted it was for the best that Walker didn't recall the trip.

"We should go back some day," Walker said, setting the album aside and focusing on Lane. He sat on the bed and snagged Lane's waist, urging him to stand between Walker's knees. "It'll be like my first time."

Lane stroked Walker's short hair that was only now beginning to grow again. "Let's wait until you get a complete bill of good health."

It was coming. Walker imagined by his next office visit, he'd get set free for a while. A smile that felt evil even to him touched Walker's lips. "Hey, look at what I can do." Walker unbuttoned Lane's jeans using only his left hand.

Lane brightened. "That's awesome, baby. Now, can you do it back?"

While keeping his expression as innocent as possible, Walker shook his head. "Sorry. That's above my skill set." Even as he made the claim, Walker slowly slid Lane's zipper down.

"We have a house full of guests." Lane's admonishment sounded breathless rather than chastising.

Walker held Lane's stare, refusing to stop. "All of which are family or like family. They know how to make themselves at home and entertain themselves. Right now, it's my job to take care of you."

Lane's gaze never wavered. "You do an amazing job of taking care of me."

Walker skimmed Lane's growing erection with his fingertips through Lane's underwear. A flush rose on Lane's cheeks. They held each other's stare, getting lost. The sound of a door snapping closed made them jump.

Lane glanced behind him, blushing. "I forgot that was open."

Walker didn't miss his chance; he shoved Lane's jeans down his hips. "Looks like we've been given permission to disappear." Walker wasn't one to pass up any chances with Lane. He knew they had the rest of their lives. Walker equally realized they should be entertaining their guests. It was Lane. They were alone and Walker lived in a constant state of need. He knew there were other couples who loved each other, but Lane and Walker had saved each other. They lived and breathed for each other. No one else understood how they fought to stay right here in each other's arms. They'd been broken down and pieced back together as one. They were soulmates. This was forever. They were home.

KEEP AN EYE OUT FOR THE NEXT BOOK IN THE series, *Sweet Baby*.

IF YOU'D LIKE TO KNOW MORE ABOUT SUMMER, I've written a short story for her. It's *Seasons*.

PLEASE CONSIDER LEAVING A REVIEW AT THE retailer where this book was purchased. Reviews really help with a book's visibility, which ensures I can continue writing. Thank you, Charity.

ABOUT THE AUTHOR

Charity Parkerson is an award winning and multi-published author with several companies. Born with no filter from her brain to her mouth, she decided to take this odd quirk and insert it in her characters.

*Eight-time Readers' Favorite Award Winner

*2015 Passionate Plume Award Finalist

*2013 Reviewers' Choice Award Winner

*2012 ARRA Finalist for Favorite Paranormal Romance

*Five-time winner of The Mistress of the Darkpath

Connect with her online:

--Join my street team: facebook.com/TeamCharityParkerson

--Sign up for my newsletter: http://bit.ly/CharityNews

--Website: charityparkerson.com

--Facebook:
facebook.com/authorCharityParkerson
facebook.com/TheMenofSin
--Twitter: twitter.com/CharityParkerso